TOM SWIFT AND HIS MOTOR CYCLE

VICTOR APPLETON

TOM SWIFT AND HIS MOTORCYCLE

OR

FUN AND ADVENTURES ON THE ROAD

The Tom Swift 100th Anniversary Rewrite Project

BY

VICTOR APPLETON

AUTHOR OF "TOM SWIFT AND HIS MOTORBOAT," "TOM SWIFT AND HIS AIRSHIP," "TOM SWIFT AND HIS SUBMARINE BOAT," ETC.

This story has been substantially rewritten in 2010 to remove overt racism toward a character of color, and to increase/modernize some of the technical and mechanical engineering concepts and action.

NEW YORK

GOOSEFAT & DEWLAP

PUBLISHERS

Made in The United States on America

Books by Victor Appleton

THE TOM SWIFT SERIES

TOM SWIFT AND HIS MOTORCYCLE
Or Fun and Adventure On The Road

TOM SWIFT AND HIS MOTORBOAT
Or the Rivals of Lake Carlopa

TOM SWIFT AND HIS AIRSHIP
Or the Stirring Cruise of the Red Cloud

TOM SWIFT AND HIS SUBMARINE BOAT
Or Under the Ocean For Sunken Treasure

TOM SWIFT AND HIS ELECTRIC RUNABOUT
Or the Speediest Car on the Road

(Other volumes in preparation)

GROSSET & DUNLAP
PUBLISHERS   NEW YORK

Tom Swift and His Motorcycle

The man appeared so quickly that Tom was
almost unable to avoid hitting him.

AUTHOR'S NOTE

The original manuscript (© 1910) included racially insensitive forms of address toward people of color, protrayed them unfavorably, and denigrated them by virtue of the patters of speech used in the book. Unlike the works of Mark Twain, by today's standards it is almost painful to read.

In addition, the sentence structure and some of the words used make in nearly unapproachable by today's youth. In order that this work not be lost, it became part of a project to rewrite the first quartet of Tom Swift books for the TOM SWIFT 100th ANNIVERSARY CONFERENCE. As such it has been heavily rewritten to the point where the new pseudononymous author (Thomas Hudson writing as Victor Appleton) now claims copyright to <u>this</u> interpretation of the work, but not the original work.

WAUKEGAN, SHOPTON & YUKAIPA
THACKERY FOX & ASSOCIATES
PUBLISHERS

Made in The United States on America

CONTENTS

TOM SWIFT and His Motorcycle

———

CHAPTER I

A NARROW ESCAPE

"THAT'S THE WAY to do it! Speed her up, Andy! Shove the spark lever over, and give her more gasoline! We'll make this a record-setting trip."

The two lads, sitting in the back seat of the touring car, currently speeding along a country road, leaned forward to speak to the youth at the steering wheel. The latter was a red-haired boy with squinty eyes and a not-very-pleasant face, but his companions seemed to regard him with much favor. Perhaps it was because they were riding in *his* automobile.

"Whoop her up, Andy!" shouted a fourth boy on the seat beside the driver. "This is immense!"

"I rather thought you'd like it," remarked Andy Foger over the noise of the engine, as he quickly turned the car to avoid a stone in the road. "Now I'll really make things hum around Shopton!"

"You have made them hum already, Andy," commented the lad beside him. "My ears are ringing. Oops! There goes my cap!"

As the boy spoke, the breeze created by the unbelievable speed at which the car was traveling lifted off his cap, and sent it whirling to the rear.

Andy Foger turned for an instant's glance behind. Then he opened the throttle still wider, and exclaimed, "Let it go, Sam. We can get another. I want to see what time I can make getting to Mansburg! I want to break a record, if I can."

"How fast are you going?" Sam asked, somewhat nervously.

"She's upwards of thirty-five miles an hour," Andy replied, a little smugly.

"Look out, or you'll break something else!" cried a lad on the rear seat. "Look out! There's a fellow on a bicycle just ahead of us. Take care, Andy!"

"Let him look out for himself," retorted Foger, as he bent lower over the steering wheel, for the car was now going more than forty miles per hour. The youth on the bicycle was riding slowly along, and did not detect the approaching automobile until it was nearly upon him. With a mean grin, Andy pressed the rubber bulb of the horn with sudden energy, sending out a series of alarming blasts.

"It's Tom Swift!" cried Sam Snedecker. "Look out, or you'll run him down!"

"Let him keep out of *my* way," retorted Andy savagely.

The youth on the bicycle, with a sudden spurt of speed, tried to cross the highway. He manage to do it, but by such a narrow margin that in sudden terror Andy Foger shut off the power, jammed down the brakes and steered crazily to one side. His heavy breaking caused the car to swerve over in a skid and went into the ditch at the side of the road where it finally stopped, tilting to one side.

Tom Swift, his face pale from his narrow escape, leaped

from his bicycle and stood regarding the automobile. Andy Foger, the driver, and his three cronies all looked very astonished and pale-faced.

"Are we—is it damaged any, Andy?" asked Sam.

"I hope not," growled Andy. "If my car's hurt it's Tom Swift's fault!"

He leaped from his seat and made a hurried inspection of the machine. He found nothing the matter, though it was more from good luck than good driving. Then, Andy turned and looked savagely at Tom Swift. The latter, standing his bicycle up against the fence, walked forward.

"What do you mean by getting in the way like that?" demanded Andy with a scowl. "Don't you see that you nearly caused a crash?"

"Well, I like your nerve, Andy Foger!" cried Tom. "What do you mean by nearly running me down? Why didn't you sound your horn sooner? You automobilists take too much for granted! You were going faster than the legal rate, anyhow!"

"I was, eh?" sneered Andy. "Bet you can't prove it!"

"Yes, you were, and you know it. If anyone, I'm the one to make an issue of this, not you. You came pretty near to hitting me. *Me* getting in *your* way! People on bicycles still have some rights on the road!"

"Aw, go on!" growled Andy. He could think of nothing else to say. "Bicycles are a back number, anyhow. Outdated. Museum pieces!"

"Well, it isn't so very long ago that you were riding one," retorted Tom. Turning to Andy's passengers he told them, "First thing you fellows know, you'll be pulled in for speeding."

"I guess we had better go slower, Andy," advised Sam in a low voice. "I don't want to be arrested."

"Leave this to me," retorted Andy. "I'm running this tour. The next time you get in my way, Swift, I'll run you down!" he threatened Tom. "Come on, fellows, we're late now and can't make a record run—all on account of him." Andy got back into the car, followed by his cronies, who had hurriedly exited the automobile after their thrilling stop.

"If you try anything like this again you'll wish you hadn't," declared Tom, and he watched the automobile party ride off.

"Oh, forget it!" snapped back Andy, and he laughed, his companions joining in with nervous laughter. They remembered Tom's threat of arrest and began to worry that he could be correct.

Tom said nothing in reply. He pulled a notebook and pencil from one pocket, then a measuring tape from another. He carefully measured the marks Andy's tires had made in the dirt as they had skidded along. He recorded the numbers and did a few computations.

Satisfied that he could now prove the speed of the reckless driver, he re-pocketed the items and turned back to his ride.

Retrieving his bicycle, he remounted and rode off, but his thoughts toward Andy Foger were not very pleasant ones. Andy was the son of a wealthy man of the town, and his father had certainly spoiled him with a dangerous combination of money and permissiveness. It had done the youth a disservice for he was a bully and a coward.

Several times he and Tom had clashed. Andy was overbearing, but seemed to require the strength he believed he had when surrounded by his "friends." This was the first time And had shown such a vindictive spirit and lack of regard for anyone's safety.

"He thinks he can run over everything since he got his new auto," muttered Tom aloud as he rode on. "He'll have a smash-up some day if he isn't careful. He's gets too much of a thrill from speeding. I wonder where he and his crowd are going?"

Musing over his narrow escape Tom rode on and was soon at his home where he lived with his widowed father, Barton Swift, a wealthy inventor. They were cared for by the latter's housekeeper, Mrs. Baggert.

Approaching a machine shop, one of several built near his house by Mr. Swift in which he conducted experiments and constructed apparatus, Tom was met by his father.

"What's the matter, Tom?" asked Mr. Swift seeing the look on Tom's face. "You look as if something has happened."

"Something very nearly did," answered the youth, and related his experience on the road.

"Humph," remarked the inventor, "your little jaunt might have ended disastrously. I suppose Andy and his friends are off on their trip. I remember Mr. Foger speaking to me about it the other day. He said Andy and some companions were going on a tour, to be gone a week or more. Well, let's all be glad it was no worse and that they are out of the area for a period. Oh, say. Have you anything special to do today, Tom?"

"No. I was just riding around for pleasure. If you want me to do anything, I'm ready."

"Then I wish you'd take this letter to Mansburg for me. I want it sent registered, and I don't wish to mail it in the Shopton post office. It's too important... it's about a valuable invention."

"Your new turbine motor, Dad?"

"That's it. On your way I wish you'd stop in Merton's machine shop and pick up some bolts he's making for me."

"I will. Is that the letter?" asked Tom extending his hand for an envelope his father held.

13

"Yes. Please be careful with it. It's to my lawyers in Washington regarding the final steps in obtaining a patent for the turbine. It is something I am creating specifically or the U.S War Department and our Navy. Very secret. That's why I'm so particular about not wanting it mailed here. Several times before I have posted letters from Shopton, only to have the information contained in them leak out before my attorneys received them. I do not want that to happen in this case. Another thing, don't speak about my new invention in Merton's shop when you stop for the bolts."

"Why? Do you think he gave out the information concerning your other work?"

"Well, not exactly. He might not mean to, but he told me the other day that some strangers were making inquiries about whether he ever did any work for me."

"What did he tell them?"

"He told them that he occasionally did, but that most of my inventive work was done in my own private shops, here. He wanted to know why the men were asking such questions, and one of them said they expected to open a machine shop in a nearby town, and wanted to see if they might count on getting any of my trade. But," he looked knowingly at Tom, "I don't believe that was their object."

"What do you think it was?"

"I don't know, exactly, but I was somewhat alarmed when I heard about it from Merton. So, I'm going to take no risks. That's why you'll send this letter from Mansburg. Don't lose it —and don't forget about the bolts. Here is a blue-print of them, so you can check to see that they come up to the specifications."

Tom rode off on his bicycle, and was soon spinning down the road.

"I wonder if I'll run into Andy Foger and his cronies again?"

he thought. "Not very likely, I guess, if they're off on a tour. Well, good. He and I always seem to get into trouble when we meet."

Tom was not destined to meet Andy again that day, but the time was to come when the red-haired bully would cause Tom Swift no little trouble, and get him into danger as well.

Tom rode along, thinking over what his father had told him about the letter he carried.

Barton Swift was a natural inventor. Even a boy he had been interested in all things mechanical, and one of his first efforts had been to arrange a system of pulleys, belts and gears so that a family windmill would operate the butter churn in the old farmhouse where he was born. The fact that the mill went so fast that it broke the churn into pieces did not discourage him, and he immediately set to work changing the gears.

His father had needed to buy a new churn, but the young inventor made his design work on the second trial. From that day on, his mother found butter-making to be almost automatic.

As he grew, Barton Swift lived in a world of inventions and dreams of inventions. People used to say he would never amount to anything—that inventors never did—but Barton proved them all wrong by amassing a considerable fortune before he reached adulthood from his many patents. He grew up, married and had one son, Tom.

Mrs. Swift died of pneumonia the winter when Tom was barely three years old, and since then the boy had lived with his father and a succession of nurses and housekeepers. The last woman to have charge of the household was Mrs. Baggert, a motherly widow. She succeeded so well, and Tom and his father formed such an attachment for her, that she was regarded as a member of the family, and had now been in charge ten years.

Mr. Swift and young Tom lived in a handsome house on the outskirts of the village of Shopton, in upper New York State. The village was near a large body of water, Lake Carlopa, and there Tom and his father used to spend many pleasant days boating. Tom and his inventor father were better friends than many boys are, and they were often seen together rowing or sailing about, or fishing. Of course, Tom had some friends his own age, but he went around with his father more often than he did with them.

Though many of Mr. Swift's inventions paid him well, and he could well-afford a more relaxed and quieter life, he was constantly seeking to perfect and develop others.

To this end, he had built several machine shops near his home with engines, lathes, machine presses and apparatus for various kinds of work.

Tom had the inventive fever running through his own veins, and had developed some useful implements and small machines as a young teenager. His father had relinquished one of the smaller workshops to his son soon after Tom's tenth birthday.

It was a fine day in April. Tom rode along the pleasant country roads on his way to Mansburg to register the letter. As he descended a little hill he saw, still some distance away but coming toward him, a great cloud of dust.

"Somebody must be driving a herd of cattle along the road," thought Tom. "I hope they don't get in my way, or, rather, I hope I don't get in theirs." He considered that it might be Andy and his cronies. "Guess I'd better keep to one side. I wish there was more room."

The dust cloud came nearer. It was so dense that whoever or whatever was making it could not be seen.

"Must be a lot of cattle in that bunch," mused the young inventor, "but I wouldn't think they'd rush them along on a warm day like this. Maybe they've stampeded. If they are I've got to look out."

This idea caused him some alarm. He glanced around trying to locate a good escape route should it become necessary. The only route open seemed to be a leap over a barbed-wire fence, which Tom did not relish needing to make.

He tried to see through the dust but could not. Nearer and nearer it came. Tom kept riding forward, taking care to remain as far to the side of the road as he could. Then, from the midst of the enveloping mass, came the sound of a steady, "chuff-chuff-chuff."

"It's a motorcycle!" exclaimed Tom. "He must have his muffler wide open, and that's what's kicking up as much dust as the wheels do. Whew! Whoever's on it will look like a clay statue at the end of his trip!"

Now that he knew it was a fellow cyclist raising such a disturbance, Tom returned to the middle of the road. He still had not had any sight of the rider, but the rhythmic explosions of the motor were nearer and louder. Tom reached for his handkerchief to cover his nose and mouth but found that he had neglected to bring one with him.

Suddenly, and just when the first advancing particles of dust reached him, making him sneeze, Tom caught sight of the rider.

He was a man of middle age, and he was clinging to the handlebars of the machine with a look of terror across his dust-crusted face. The motor was running at full speed.

Tom quickly turned to one side to avoid the worst of the dust. The motorcyclist glanced at the youth, but this act nearly proved disastrous for him. He took his eyes off of the road for just a moment and did not see a large stone directly in his path. His front wheel hit it, and the heavy machine—

which he seemed barely able to control—skidded over toward Tom. The motorcyclist bounced up in the air from the saddle, losing his footing on the pegs, and nearly lost his hold on the handlebars.

"Look out!" cried Tom shoving his bicycle out of harm's way. "You'll smash into me!"

"I—I'm—try—ing—not—to!" were the words that rattled out of the middle-aged man.

Tom gave his bicycle a final, desperate twist to get out of the way. The motorcyclist tried to do the same, but the machine now appeared to have a mind of its own. It came straight for Tom, and a disastrous collision might have resulted had it not skidded off another stone in the road. The front wheel hit it and the entire motorcycle swerved to one side. It flashed past Tom, just grazing his rear wheel, and then was lost to sight beyond in a cloud of dust that seemed to follow it like a halo.

"Why don't you learn to ride before you come out on the road!" cried out Tom somewhat angrily.

Floating back like an echo from the dust-cloud came, "I'm—try—ing—to!" Then the sound of the explosions became fainter and were soon lost.

"Well, he's got lots to learn yet!" exclaimed Tom trying to beat the dust from his clothes and hair. "That's twice today I've nearly been run down. I expect I'd better look out for the third time. They say that's always fatal," and the lad leaped from his vehicle.

"Wonder if he bent any of my spokes?" the young inventor continued as he bent down to inspect his dusty bicycle.

TOM SWIFT and His Motorcycle

———

CHAPTER II

TOM OVERHEARS SOMETHING

"EVERYTHING SEEMS to be all right," Tom remarked, "but another inch or so and he'd have crashed into me. I wonder who he was?" Tom looked to where the man and machine had disappeared. "I wish I had a machine like that. I could make better time than I can on my bicycle. Perhaps I'll get one some day." He sighed. "Well, I might as well ride on."

Tom was soon at Mansburg and the local post office where he handed in the letter for mailing. He looked about to see if there were any suspicious characters. The only person he noticed was a well-dressed man, with a black mustache and bowler-style hat, who seemed to be intently studying the delivery schedules.

"Do you want the delivery receipt for the registered letter sent to you here or at Shopton?" the clerk asked Tom. "Come to think of it, though, it will have to come here. You can call back for it. I'll have it returned to Mr. Barton Swift, care of general delivery, and you can pick it up the next time you are over," he suggested.

"That will do," answered Tom. As he turned away he saw that the man who had been inquiring about the mails was regarding him curiously. Tom thought nothing of it at the time, but there came an occasion when he wished that he had taken more careful note of the well-dressed individual. As the youth passed through the outer door he saw the man walk over to the registry window.

"He seems to have considerable mail business," thought Tom, and then the matter passed from his mind as he mounted his bicycle and hurried to the machine shop.

"Say, I'm awfully sorry, Tom," announced Mr. Merton when Tom said he had come for the bolts, "but they're not quite done. They need polishing. I know I promised them to your father today, and he will have them, but he was very particular about the polish, and one of my best workers was taken sick. I'm a little behind."

"How long will it take to polish them?" asked Tom.

"Oh, about an hour. In fact, a man is working on them now. If you could call back this afternoon they'll be ready. Can you?"

"I suppose I've got to," replied Tom good-naturedly. "I'll have to stay in Mansburg for lunch. I can't get back to Shopton in time now."

"I'll be sure to have them for you after lunch," promised Mr. Merton. "Now, there's a matter I want to speak to you about, Tom. Has your father any thoughts of giving the work he has been turning over to me to some other firm?"

"Not that I know of. Why?" Tom replied, looking puzzled.

"Well, I'll tell you why. Some time ago there was a stranger in here, asking about your father's work. I told Mr. Swift of it at the time. The stranger said then that he and some others were thinking of opening a machine shop a few miles from here, and he wanted to know whether they would be likely to get any jobs from your father. I told the man I knew nothing about your father's business, and he went away. I didn't hear any more of it. Of course, I don't want to lose your father's trade. Then a funny thing happened. Just this morning that very same man was back here, and he was making particular inquiries about your father's private machine shops."

"He was?" exclaimed Tom excitedly.

"Yes. He wanted to know where they were located, how they were laid out, and what sort of work he did in them."

"What did you tell him?"

"Nothing at all. I suspected something, and I said the best way for him to find out would be to go and see your father. Wasn't that right?"

"Sure. Dad doesn't want his business known any more than he can help. What do you suppose they wanted?"

"Well, the man talked as though he and his partners might like to buy your father's shops."

"He'd never sell. First, they are on our property. He has them arranged just for his own use. Everything set just so he can turn out his prototypes and register them for patents. I'm sure he would not get rid of them."

"Well, that's what I thought, but I didn't tell the man so. I judged it would be best for him to find out for himself."

"What was the man's name?"

"He didn't tell me, and I didn't ask him."

"How did he look?"

"Gee, he was well dressed, wore kid gloves and all that, and he had a little black mustache."

Tom started, and Mr. Merton noticed it.

"Do you know him?" he asked.

"No," replied Tom, "but I saw—" Then he stopped. He recalled the man he had seen in the post office. He answered this description, but it was too vague to be certain.

"Did you say you'd seen him?" asked Mr. Merton, regarding Tom curiously.

"No—yes—that is—well, I'll tell my father about it," stammered Tom, who concluded that it would be best to say nothing of his suspicions. "I'll be back right after lunch, Mr. Merton. Please have the bolts ready for me, if you can."

"I will. Is your father going to use them in some new machine?"

"Oh, dad is always making new machines," answered the youth, as the most polite way of not giving the proprietor of the shop any information. "I'll be back in one hour," he called as he went out to get on his bicycle.

Tom was very puzzled. He felt certain that the man in the post office and the one who had questioned Mr. Merton were the same.

"There is something going on, that dad should know about," reflected Tom. "I must tell him. Maybe he shouldn't send any more of his patent work over to Merton until this mystery is solved. We can do it in our shops, and dad and I will have to keep our eyes open. There may be spies about seeking to discover something about his new turbine motor. I'll hurry back with those bolts and tell dad. But first I must get lunch. I'll go to the restaurant and have a good feed while I'm stuck here."

Tom had plenty of spending money, some of which came from a small patent he had marketed himself for a device to wind pocket watches, based on how much tension was left in the spring. He left his bicycle outside the restaurant, first taking the precaution to chain the wheels to a lamp post, and then went inside.

Tom was hungry and ordered a good meal. He was about half way through it when someone called his name.

"Hello, Ned!" he answered, looking up to see a youth about his own age. "Where did you blow in from?"

"Oh, I came over from Shopton this morning," replied Ned Newton, taking a seat at the table with Tom. The two boys were friends, and in their younger days had often gone fishing, swimming and hunting together. Now, Ned worked in the Shopton bank, and Tom was busy helping his father, so they did not see each other as often.

"On business or pleasure?" asked Tom, putting some sugar in his coffee.

"Business. I had to bring some papers over from our bank to the First National here. What about you?"

"Oh, I came on dad's account."

"Invented anything new?" asked Ned as he gave his order to the waitress.

"No, nothing notable since the egg-beater I was telling you about. But I'm working on some things."

"Why don't you invent a flying automobile or a high-speed airship?"

"Maybe I will some day, but, speaking of autos... did you see the one Andy Foger has?"

"Yes. It's a beaut! Too bad he owns it. Have you seen it?"

"Altogether at too close range. He nearly ran over me this morning," and the young inventor related the occurrence.

"Oh, Andy always was a jerk," commented Ned, "and now his father let him get the touring car I suppose he'll be worse than ever."

"Well, if he tries to run me down again he'll get into trouble," declared Tom, calling for a second cup of coffee.

The two friends began conversing on more congenial topics, and Ned was soon telling Tom of a new camera he had. As Ned was describing the viewfinder, Tom heard some one in the booth behind him remark in rather loud tones, "The plant is located in Shopton, all right, and the buildings are near Swift's house. Maybe too close."

Tom motioned Ned to continue talking while he turned his head slightly and listened more intently.

"That will make it more difficult," one man stated. "But if that invention is as valuable as—"

"Shhhh!" came a caution from another of the party. "This is too public a place to discuss the matter. Wait until we get outside. One of us will have to see Swift, of course, and if he proves stubborn—"

"I guess you'd better hush yourself," retorted the man who had first spoken, and then the voices subsided.

But Tom had overheard things that made him vaguely afraid. He was so started at the mention of his father's name that he had knocked a fork from the table.

"What's the matter, getting nervous?" asked Ned with a laugh.

"I guess so," replied Tom, and went to pick the fork up, stealing a look at the strangers behind him. He was startled to note that one of them was the man from the post office—the man who also answered the description of the one inquiring of Mr. Merton about the Swift shops.

"I've got to keep my ears open," thought Tom as he went back to eating his food.

TOM SWIFT and His Motorcycle

———

CHAPTER III

IN A SMASH-UP

THOUGH THE young inventor listened intently in an endeavor to hear the conversation of the men at the table behind him, all he could catch was an indistinct murmur. The strangers appeared to have heeded the caution of one of their number and were speaking in low tones.

Tom and Ned finished their meal, and started to leave the restaurant. As Tom passed the men at their table, they looked up quickly at him. Two of them gave Tom only a passing glance, but one—the man he had noticed in the post office—stared long and intently.

"I think he will recognize me the next time he sees me," thought Tom and boldly returned the stare of the stranger.

The specialty bolts were ready when he called at the machine shop the second time. He fastened the package of them to the saddle of his bicycle and started for home at a fast pace. He was just turning from a cross road into the main highway when he spotted a woman driving a light wagon ahead of him. She appeared more intent on the scenery around her than on driving the wagon.

When the sun flashed on Tom's shining bicycle frame it flashed onto her horse. The horse gave a sudden start and a leap—pulling the reins from her hands—then swerved to one side, and bolted down the dusty stretch. The woman was screaming at the top of her voice.

"A runaway!" cried Tom

Without waiting an instant, the lad bent over his handlebars and pedaled with all his might. His bicycle seemed fairly to leap forward after the galloping horse.

"Sit still! Don't jump out! Don't jump!" yelled the young inventor to the frightened woman. "I'll try to catch him!" He has seen that the woman was standing up in front of the seat and leaning forward, as if about to leap from the wagon.

"She's lost her head," thought Tom. "No wonder! That's a skittish horse."

Faster and faster he rode, bending all his energies to overtake the animal. The wagon was swaying from side to side, with one or another wheel raising from the road. More than once, the woman just saved herself from being thrown out by grasping the edge of the seat. Finally figuring out that standing up was dangerous, she crouched in the bottom of the swaying vehicle.

"That's better!" shouted Tom, but thought it doubtful that she heard him, for the rattling of the wagon and the hoofbeats of the horse drowned all other sounds. "Sit still!" he shouted. "I'll stop the horse for you!"

Trying to imagine himself in a desperate race in order to excite himself to greater speed, Tom continued gaining. He came even with the tail-board of the wagon, and was still creeping up. The woman was all huddled up in a lump.

"Grab the reins! Grab the reins!" shouted Tom. "Pull back on the reins! That will stop him!"

The occupant of the wagon turned to look at the lad. Tom got the impression that she was an attractive young lady. "Grab the reins!" he cried again. "Pull hard!"

"I—I can't!" she answered, terror filling her voice. "They fell down! Oh, please stop the horse! I'm so—so frightened!"

"I'll stop him!" declared the youth firmly, and he set his teeth hard. Then he saw the reason the pretty driver could not grasp the lines. They had slipped over the dashboard and were trailing on the ground.

The horse was slowing a bit now, as the fast pace was winding the animal normally use to a more sedate speed of travel. Tom saw his opportunity, and with a sudden burst of energy was at the animal's head.

Steering his bicycle with one hand, Tom made a grab for the reins near the bit. This action frightened the horse and it pulled its head to one side, but Tom swung in the same direction. He grasped the leather and then, with a kick, freed himself from the bicycle, giving it a shove to one side. He was now clinging to the reins with both hands. Being a muscular lad and no lightweight, his presence registered on the horse's brain.

"Sit—still!" panted our hero to the young woman, who had arisen to the seat. "I'll have him stopped in half a minute now!"

It was in less time than that, the horse, finding it impossible to shake off Tom's grip, began to slow from a gallop to a trot, then to a canter, and finally to a slow walk. A moment later the horse stopped, breathing heavily from its run. It turned to look at Tom and blew its nose in his direction to register its displeasure.

"There, there, now!" spoke Tom soothingly, patting it softly

27

on the muzzle. "You're all right, old fellow. I hope you're not hurt," he said to the young lady. Tom went to make a motion to raise his cap, only to find that it had blown off.

"Oh, no—no, I'm more frightened than hurt."

"It was my fault," declared the young inventor. "I should not have swung into the road so suddenly. My bicycle scared your horse."

"Yes, Old Bert is easily disturbed," admitted the fair driver. "He apparently hates bright lights. And dogs. And lots of other things. I can't thank you enough for stopping him. You saved me from a terrible accident."

"It was the least I could do. Are you all right now?" and he handed up the dangling reins. "I think Old Bert, as you call him, has had enough of running," added Tom looking at the animal who now stood quietly.

"I do hope so. Yes, I am all right. I trust your bicycle is not damaged. If it is, my father, Mr. Amos Nestor, of New York City, will gladly pay for its repair."

This reminded the young inventor of his bicycle. Making sure that the horse would not start up again, he trotted back to where his bicycle and his cap lay. He found that the only damage to the bicycle was a few bent spokes. After straightening them and having again apologized to the young woman—receiving in return her pardon and thanks. Before parting, she told him that her name was Mary Nestor, and that she was visiting her cousin.

"Perhaps we will see each other again. Hopefully, under less dire circumstances," she remarked before mentioning that she needed to get on with her trip.

Tom once more resumed his trip. The wagon followed him at a distance, the horse displaying no desire now to move beyond a slow amble.

"Well, things are certainly happening to me today," mused Tom as he pedaled on. "That might have led to a serious accident if there'd been anything in the road."

Tom did not stop to consider that he had been instrumental in preventing a bad accident, as he believed he had been the innocent cause of starting the runaway. But, Tom was ever a modest lad. His arms were sore from jerking on the bridle, but he did not mind that much, and bent over the handlebars to make up for lost time.

As he pulled away from the wagon, he raised a hand and waved back to the young woman.

He was within a short distance of his house and coasting easily along when, just ahead of him, he saw a cloud of dust very similar to the one that had concealed the inexperienced motorcyclist earlier in the day.

"I wonder if that's him again?" thought Tom. "If it is, I'm going to hang back until I see which way he's headed. No use running any more risks."

At that moment, a puff of wind blew some of the dust to one side. Tom had a glimpse of the man on the puffing machine.

"It's the same man!" he exclaimed aloud, "and he's going the same way I am. Well, I'll not try to catch up to him. I wonder what he's been doing all this while, that he hasn't gotten any farther than this? Either he's been riding back and forth, or else he stopped for a long rest. My, but he certainly is scooting along!" he said thinking how wonderful it would be to own such a vehicle.

The wind carried the sound of the explosions of the motor, and he could see the man clinging tightly to the handlebars. The rider was almost in front of Tom's house now, when, with a suddenness that caused the lad to utter an exclamation of alarm, the stranger turned his machine right toward a big oak tree.

"What's he up to?" cried Tom excitedly. "Does he plan to climb that, or is he out of control again?"

A moment later, one side of the motorcycle struck the tree a glancing blow.

The man went flying over the handlebars, the machine was heading to the ditch along the road, and falling over on one side. The motor suddenly raced furiously. The rider lay in a heap at the foot of the tree.

"Oh, dear!" cried Tom. "He must be killed!" and bending forward, he raced toward the scene of the accident.

TOM SWIFT and His Motorcycle

———

CHAPTER IV

A BOY AND A MOTORCYCLE

WHEN TOM reached the figure laying on the grass at the foot of the old oak tree, he bent quickly over the man. There was an ugly cut on his forehead, and blood was flowing from it. But Tom quickly noticed that the stranger was breathing, though not very strongly.

"Well, he's not dead—not yet!" exclaimed the youth with a sigh of relief. "But I guess he's pretty badly hurt. I must get help—no, I'll take him into our house. It's not far. I'll call dad."

Tom pressed his handkerchief against the wound for a moment while he looked for signs of broken bones. Finally, he picked the man's hand up and set it atop the makeshift bandage. "It will have to do," he thought.

He got up.

Leaning his wheel against the tree Tom started to run for his house, about three hundred feet away before noticing that the stranger's motorcycle was running at full speed on the ground.

"I'd better shut off the power!" he exclaimed. "No use letting the machine be ruined." Tom had a natural love for machinery, and it hurt him almost as much to see a piece of fine apparatus abused as it did to see an animal mistreated. In just a moment he shut off the gasoline and spark. Only then did the youth race on toward his house.

"Where's dad?" he called to Mrs. Baggert as he dashed into the house.

"Out in one of the shops," replied the housekeeper, looking up from her dishes. "Why, Tom," she went on hurriedly as she saw how excited he was, "whatever has happened?"

"Man hurt—out in front—motorcycle smash—I'm going to bring him in here—get some things ready—bandages—I'll find dad!" Tom was out of breath more from the excitement than from the run.

"Bless and save us all!" cried Mrs. Baggert. "Whatever are we coming to? Who's hurt? How did it happen? Is he dead?"

"Haven't time to talk now," answered Tom, rushing back out of the house. "Dad and I will bring him in here."

Tom found his father in one of the three small machine shops on the grounds about the Swift home. The youth hurriedly told what had happened.

"Of course we'll bring him right in here!" assented Mr. Swift, putting aside the work upon which he was engaged and wiping his hands. "Did you tell Mrs. Baggert?"

"Yes, and she's all in a dither."

"Well, she can't help it, being a woman, I suppose. But we'll manage. Do you know the man?"

"Never saw him before today, until he tried to run me down. Accidentally, I'm sure. Guess he doesn't know much about motorcycles. But come on, Dad. He may bleed to death."

Father and son hurried to where the stranger lay. As they bent over him he opened his eyes and asked faintly, "Where am I? What happened?"

"You're all right—you're in good hands," said Mr. Swift. "Are you much hurt?"

The man took his hand and Tom's handkerchief away from his face and, seeing the blood, blanched white. "Uh—Not much—mostly stunned, I think. What happened?" he repeated looking from them to the bloody piece of linen and back.

"You and your motorcycle tried to climb a tree," remarked Tom with grim humor.

"Oh, yes, I remember now. I couldn't seem to steer out of the way. And I couldn't shut off the power in time. Is the motorcycle badly damaged?"

"The front wheel is," reported Tom, glancing at the machine sitting in the nearby ditch, "and there are some other breaks, but I guess—"

"How unfortunate. I wish it was *all* smashed!" exclaimed the man vigorously. "I never want to see that infernal device again!"

"Why, don't you like it?" asked Tom. Secretly, he had a sudden wish that the man would not want to retrieve the motorcycle and that Tom might have it to tinker with.

"No. I never have, and I never will," the man spoke faintly but determinedly.

"Never mind now," interposed Mr. Swift. "Don't excite yourself. My son and I will take you to our house and send for a doctor."

"I'll bring the motorcycle to the house, after we've carried you in," added Tom.

"Don't worry about the machine. I never want to see it again!" went on the man, rising himself to a sitting position. "It nearly killed me twice today. I swear I'll never ride again."

"You'll feel differently after the doctor fixes you up," said Mr. Swift with a smile.

"Doctor! I don't need a doctor," cried the stranger. "I am only bruised and shaken up. A doctor, indeed!"

"You have a bad cut on your head," said Tom.

"It isn't very deep," went on the injured man, touching it with his fingers and examining the blood. "Fortunately I struck the tree a glancing blow. If you will allow me to rest in your house a little while and give me a bandage plaster for the cut and a glass of water I shall be all right again."

"Can you walk, or shall we carry you?" asked Tom's father.

"I think I can walk, if you'll support me a little." And the stranger proved that he could do this by getting to his feet and taking a few shaky steps. Mr. Swift and his son took gentle hold of his arms and led him to the house. There he was placed on a lounge and given some simple restoratives by Mrs. Baggert, who, when she found the accident was not serious, rapidly recovered her composure.

She was able to take Tom's bloodied handkerchief away without making too much of a fuss.

"I must have been unconscious for a few minutes," went on the man. "I don't remember a thing from the moment I bounced off of that tree until you were bending over me."

"You were," explained Tom. "When I got up to you I thought you were dead, until I saw you breathing. Then I shut off the power of your machine and ran in for dad. I've got the motorcycle outside. You can't ride it for some time, I'm afraid, Mr.—er—" and Tom stopped in some confusion, for he realized that they did not know the man's name.

"I beg your pardon for not introducing myself before," said the stranger. "I'm Wakefield Damon, of Waterfield. But don't worry about me riding that machine again. I never shall."

"Oh, perhaps—" began Mr. Swift.

"No, I never shall," went on Mr. Damon positively, nodding his head to punctuate the statement. "My doctor told me to get it. *He* thought riding around the country in fresh air would benefit my health. Hah! I shall tell him his prescription nearly killed me."

"And me too," added Tom with a laugh.

"How—why—you aren't the young man I nearly ran down this morning?" asked Mr. Damon, suddenly sitting up and looking at the youth.

"I am," answered Tom, with a grin.

"Bless my soul! So you are!" cried Mr. Damon. "I was wondering who it could be. It's quite a coincidence. But I was in such a cloud of dust I couldn't make out who it was."

"You had your muffler open, and that made considerable dust blowing all down onto the dirt," explained Tom.

"Was that it? Bless my existence! I *thought* something was wrong, but I couldn't tell what. I went over all the instructions in the book and what the sales agent told me, but I couldn't think of the right solution. I tried all sorts of things to make less dust, but I couldn't. Then, bless my eyelashes, if the machine didn't stop just after I nearly ran into you. I pulled into a side road and had to tinker with it for an hour or more before I could get it to going again. Then I ran into the tree. My doctor told me the machine would do my liver good, but, bless my happiness, I'd as soon be without a liver entirely as to do what I've done today. I am through and done with motorcycling!"

A hopeful look came over Tom's face, but he said nothing.

In a little while Mr. Damon felt so much better that he said he would like to start for home. "I'm afraid you'll have to leave your machine here," said Tom.

"You can send for it any time you want to," added Mr. Swift.

"Bless my hatband!" exclaimed Mr. Damon, who appeared to be very fond of blessing his various organs and his articles of wearing apparel. "Bless my hatband! Have you not listened to a word I've said? I never want to see it again! If you will be so kind as to just keep it for me, I will send a junk man after it. I will never spend anything on having it repaired. I am done with that form of exercise—liver or no liver—doctor or no doctor."

He appeared very determined. Tom quickly made up his mind. Mr. Damon had gone to the bathroom to get rid of some of the mud on his hands and face.

"Father," said Tom earnestly, "may I buy that machine of his?"

"What? Buy a broken motorcycle?"

"I can easily fix it. It comes from a well-respected company and is a fine make. In spite of the recent event, it is in good condition. It's practically new. I can repair it. I've wanted a motorcycle for some time, and here's a chance to get a good one cheap."

"You don't need to do that," replied Mr. Swift. "You have money enough to buy a new one if you want it. I never knew you cared for them."

"I didn't, until lately. But I'd rather buy this one and fix it up than get a new one. Besides, I have an idea for improvements such as a new kind of transmission and sparker. Perhaps I can work those out on this machine."

"Oh, well, if you want it for experimental purposes, I suppose it will be as good as any. Go ahead, get it if you wish, but don't give him too much for it."

"I'll not. I fancy I can get it cheap."

Mr. Damon returned to the living room, where he had first been carried. He had cleaned himself up and now sported only a small bandage plaster on his forehead.

"I cannot thank you enough for what you have done for me," he said. "I might have lain there for hours. Bless my very existence! I have had a very narrow escape. Hereafter when I see anyone on a motorcycle I shall turn my head away. The memory will be too painful," and he touched the plaster that covered the cut on his head.

"Mr. Damon," said Tom quickly, "will you sell me that motorcycle?"

"Bless my finger rings! Sell you that mass of junk?"

"It really isn't all junk," went on the young inventor. "I believe that I can fix it, though, of course," he added prudently, "it will cost me something. How much would you want for it?"

"Well," replied Mr. Damon, "I paid two hundred and fifty dollars last week. I have ridden a hundred miles on it. That is at the rate of two dollars and a half a mile—pretty expensive riding. But, if you are in earnest I will let you have the machine for fifty dollars, and then I fear that I will be taking advantage of you. Do you still want it?"

"Yes. I'll give you fifty dollars," said Tom quickly. "Deal?"

Mr. Damon exclaimed, "Bless my liver—that is, if I still have one. Do you mean it?"

Tom nodded. "I'll fetch you the money right away," he said, starting for his room.

He retrieved the cash from a small safe to which he had fitted an ingenious burglar alarm, and was on his way downstairs when he heard his father call out, "Here! What do you want? Go away from that shop! No one is allowed there!" and looking from an upper window, Tom saw his father running toward a stranger, who was just stepping from the shop where Mr. Swift was constructing his turbine motor.

Tom started as he saw that the stranger was the same black-mustached man whom he had noticed in the post office, and, later, in the restaurant at Mansburg.

TOM SWIFT and His Motorcycle

—

CHAPTER V

MR. SWIFT IS ALARMED

STUFFING THE money he intended to give to Mr. Damon in his pocket, Tom ran downstairs. As he passed through the living room, intending to see what the disturbance was about —and, if necessary, aid his father—the owner of the broken motorcycle exclaimed, "What's the matter? What has happened? Bless my coat tails, but is anything wrong?"

"I don't know," answered Tom. "There is a stranger in my father's work shop, and he *never* allows that. I'll be back in a minute."

"Take your time," advised the somewhat eccentric Mr. Damon. "I find my legs are a bit weaker than I suspected, and I will be glad to rest a while longer. Bless my shoelaces, but don't hurry!"

Tom ran into the rear yard where the shops, a small cluster of buildings, were located. He saw his father confronting the man with the black mustache, and Mr. Swift was saying:

"What do you want? This is not public property. I allow no

people to come in here unless I or my son invites them. Did you wish to see me?"

"Are you Mr. Barton Swift?" asked the man.

"Yes, that is my name."

"The inventor of the Swift safety lamp, and the turbine motor?"

At the mention of the motor Mr. Swift started.

"I am the inventor of the safety lamp you mention," he said stiffly, "but I must decline to talk about any motor. May I ask where you obtained your information concerning it?"

"Why, I am not at liberty to tell," went on the man. "I called to see if we could negotiate with you for the sale of it. Parties whom I represent—"

At that moment Tom plucked his father by the sleeve.

"Dad," whispered the youth, "I saw him in Mansburg. I think he is one of several who have been inquiring in Mr. Merton's shop about you and your patents. I wouldn't have anything to do with him until I found out more about him."

"Is that so?" asked Mr. Swift quickly. Then, turning to the stranger, he said: "My son tells me—"

But Mr. Swift got no further, for at that moment the stranger caught sight of Tom, whom he had not noticed before.

"Oh!" exclaimed the man. "I have forgotten something—an important engagement, that is—will be back directly—will see you again, Mr. Swift—excuse the trouble I have put you to—I am in a great hurry," and before father or son could stop him, the man turned and walked quickly from the yard.

Mr. Swift stood staring at him, and so did Tom. Then the inventor asked, "Do you know that man? What about him, Tom? Why did he leave so hurriedly?"

"I don't know his name," replied Tom, "but I am suspicious of him, and I think he left because he recognized me." He told his father of seeing the man in the post office, and hearing him talk to his two companions in the restaurant.

In the distance they heard an automobile starting up and speeding away.

"And so you think they are up to some mischief, Tom?" asked the inventor when the son had finished.

"Well, I wouldn't go quite as far as that, but I think they are interested in your patents, and you ought to know whether you want them to be, or not."

"I most certainly do not—especially in the turbine motor. That is my latest invention and will, I think, prove very valuable. Though I have not mentioned it before, I expected to have some trouble because of it."

He explained to Tom that the new turbine had been designed to meet a military need.

Several of the nations in Europe had been making overtures of invasion or even war toward their less-armed neighbors. At least one of the aggressor nations already had a small fleet of underwater marine craft, or submarines, capable of delivering an explosive torpedo into the underside of any naval ship.

"Or worse, they might decide to attach a non-military ship. So, I have designed and constructed a special turbine motor that will operate under water, without the aid of air. It uses a new fuel the Navy has designed that burns to create its own oxygen."

Tom was amazed and told his father just that. "I can see why spies might try to steal your designs," he told the older man, "but why would someone who appears to be from our very own country want to do so?"

"Soon after I perfected it, with the exception of some minor details, I received word from a syndicate of rich men that I was infringing on a previously-designed motor, the patent of which they controlled. This surprised me for two reasons. One was because I did not know that any one knew I had invented the motor. I had kept the matter very secret, and I am at a loss to know how it leaked out. To prevent any further information concerning my plans becoming public, I sent you to Mansburg today. But now it seems that the precaution was of little avail. Another matter of surprise was the information that I was infringing on the patent of someone else. I had a very careful examination made, and I found that the syndicate of rich men is wrong. I am not infringing. In fact, although the motor they have is somewhat like mine, there is one big difference—*theirs does not work*, while mine does. Their patents are worthless."

"Then what do you think is their object?"

"I think they want to get control of my turbine motor, Tom. That is what has been worrying me lately. I know these men to be unscrupulous, and, with plenty of money, they may make trouble for me. What also upsets me is that at least two of the syndicate men have direct ties with the governments of European nations."

"But can't you get the U.S. Government involved. And can't you fight them in the courts?"

"Yes, I could do that. It is not as if I was a poor man, but I do not like lawsuits. I want to live quietly and invent things. I dislike litigation. However, if they force it on me I will fight!" exclaimed Mr. Swift determinedly. "As to the government, they have warned me that they wish no notoriety regarding their plans for a torpedo to feature my turbine. They feel that such news might tip their hand,"

"Do you think this man was one of the crowd of financiers?" asked Tom.

"It would be hard to say. I did not like his actions, and the fact that he sneaked in here as if he was trying to steal or possibly photograph some of my models or plans, makes me very suspicious."

"It certainly does," agreed Tom. "Now, if we only knew his name we could—"

He suddenly paused and sprang forward. He picked up an envelope that had dropped where the stranger had been standing.

"The man lost this from his pocket, Dad," said Tom eagerly. "It's a telegram. Shall we look at it?"

"I think we are entirely justified in protecting ourselves. Is the envelope already open?"

"Yes."

"Then read the telegram. I'd say that it is fair game."

Tom drew out a folded yellow slip of paper. It was a short message.

He read:

> Amberson Morse, Mansburg.
> See Swift today. Make offer. If not
> accepted do the best you can. Spare
> no effort. Plans must be securred.

"Is that all?" asked Mr. Swift.

"All except the signature."

"Who is the telegram signed by?"

"By Elrod & Drimble," answered Tom.

"Those rascally lawyers!" exclaimed his father. "I was beginning to suspect this. That is the firm which represents the syndicate of wealthy men who are trying to get my turbine motor patents away from me. Tom, we must be on our guard! They will wage a fierce fight against me. They have invested many thousands of dollars in a worthless machine and are desperate."

"We'll fight 'em!" cried Tom. "You and I, Dad! We'll show them that the firm of Swift & Son is swift by name and swift by nature!"

"Good!" exclaimed the inventor. "I'm glad you feel that way about it, Tom. But we are going to have no easy task. Those men are rich and totally unscrupulous. We shall have to be on guard constantly. Let me have that telegram. It may come in useful. Now I must send word to Reid & Crawford, my attorneys in Washington, to be on the lookout. I believe that I also must make contact with people in Washington D.C. They must be made aware of the seriousness of our situation. Matters are coming to a curious pass."

As Mr. Swift and his son started for the house, they met Mr. Damon coming toward them.

"Bless my very existence!" cried the eccentric man. "I was beginning to fear something had happened to you. I am glad that you are all right. I heard voices, then that man all but ran past your sitting room window, and I imagined—"

"It's all right," Mr. Swift reassured him. "There was a stranger about my shop, and I never allow that. Do you feel well enough to go? If not we shall be glad to have you remain with us for the evening and night. We have plenty of room."

"Oh, thank you very much, but I must be going. I feel much better. Bless my gaiters, but I never will trust myself in any automotive contraption again! I will renounce gasoline from now on."

"That reminds me," spoke Tom. "I have the money for the motorcycle," and he drew out the bills. "You are sure you will not regret your bargain, Mr. Damon? The machine is almost new, and needs only slight repairs. Fifty dollars is—"

"Tut, tut, young man! I feel as if I was getting the best of you. Bless my handkerchief! I hope you have no bad luck with it."

"I'll try and be careful," promised Tom with a smile as he handed over the money. "I am going to gear it differently and put some improvements on it. Then I will use it instead of my bicycle. You mentioned a book of instructions. Do you have it or might I come collect it sometime?"

Mr. Damon patted his pockets. "Oh, bless my empty head. Of course I don't have it with me. It is to be found in a compartment just under the seat. Yes. I daresay that is exactly where I placed it this very day."

Tom thanked the gentleman.

"It will need to be very much improved before ever I trusted myself on it again," declared Mr. Damon. "Well, I appreciate what you have done for me, and if at any time I can reciprocate the favor, I will only be too glad to do so. Bless my soul, though, I hope I don't have to rescue you from trying to climb a tree," and with a laugh, which showed that he had fully recovered from his mishap, he shook hands with father and son and left on foot.

"A very nice but rather odd man, Tom," commented Mr. Swift. "Somewhat out of the ordinary, but a very fine character, for all that is my assessment of him."

"That's what I say," added the son. "Now, Dad, you'll soon see me scooting around the country on my motorcycle. I've always wanted one, and now I have a bargain."

"Do you think you can repair it?"

"Of course, Dad. I've done more difficult things than that. I'm going to take it apart now, and see what it needs."

"Before you do that, Tom, I wish you would take a pair of telegrams to town for me. I must wire my lawyers and the governmental department of the Navy at once."

Tom promised him to do so as soon as Barton Swift could provide him with the written messages.

"Oh, and Son. Here is a five dollar note. Please stop by the general hardware store and procure some new padlocks and extra strong hasps for me. I intend to lock my work shops up as securely as possible before the evening comes."

"Dad looks worried," thought Tom as he wheeled the broken motorcycle into the smallest of the Swift machine shops, where he did most of his work. "Well, I don't blame him. But we'll get the best of those scoundrels yet!"

Tom had a small sandwich of chopped liver and onions provided by Mrs. Baggert. "Young boys need liver," she exclaimed as he hesitantly took the plate from her. It seemed to be Mrs. Baggert's remedy for all sorts of imagined ills and was something Tom rarely looked forward to.

He was saved from eating the second half of the sandwich by his father who came into the kitchen and handed Tom two different pieces of paper.

"Just don't get them confused," he requested.

Tom grinned at his father, took one final gulp of milk, and left the house by the back door.

As he climbed aboard his bicycle, his father leaned out of the door and called to him. "You be extra careful, Son. Keep an eye out for those mysterious men!"

TOM SWIFT and His Motorcycle

————

CHAPTER VI

AN INTERVIEW IN THE DARK

WHILE TOM was riding to the village, he mentally inspected the motorcycle he had purchased. Tom believed that a few repairs easy would suffice to put it back into ridable shape, though an entire new front wheel would be needed. He was certain that the motor had not been damaged thanks to his quick action is shutting it down. Tom rode on into the village of Shopton. As he hurried along he noticed in the west a bank of ugly-looking clouds that indicated a shower.

"I'm in for a wetting before I get back," he mused, and he increased his speed, reaching the telegraph office shortly before four o'clock.

"Think this storm will hold off until I get home?" asked Tom the telegrapher.

"I'm afraid not," answered the agent. "Had a wire come in warning of a storm coming in over Old Forge right this minute. Could be here in less than a half hour I reckon. We'd better get a hustle on."

Because Barton had asked Tom to bring back a receipt for the telegrams, he needed to wait until the man had keyed them in and had received notification they had been received.

The telegrapher quickly wrote out the receipt and handed it to the youth. "Scoot along not, Tom," he suggested.

Tom sprinted off. Outside, he unchained his bicycle and began pedaling out of town. It was rapidly getting dark as clouds now completely covered the sky. When he was still about a mile from home he felt several warm drops on his face.

"Here it comes!" exclaimed the youth. "Now for a little more speed!"

Tom pressed harder on the pedals, too hard, in fact, for an instant later something snapped, and the next he knew he was flying over the handlebars of the bicycle. At the same time there was a metallic, clinking sound.

"Chain's busted!" exclaimed the lad as he picked himself up out of the dampening dust. "Well, doesn't that just take the cake!" and he walked back to where, in the cloud-induced dusk, he could dimly discern his bicycle.

The chain had come off the two sprockets and was lying to one side. Tom picked it up and discovered by close observation that the screw and nut holding the two joining links together was lost.

"Nice pickle!" he murmured. "How am I going to find it in all this dust and darkness?" he asked himself disgustedly. "I'll carry an extra screw next time. No, I won't, either. I'll ride my motorcycle next time. Well, I may as well give a look around. I hate to walk, if I can fix it and ride."

Tom had not spent more than two minutes looking about the dusty road with the aid of matches when the rain suddenly began falling in a hard shower.

He spend several additional minutes patting the dirt in a vain attempt to locate the missing screw and nut. Twice he found small stones he mistook for the nut. Finally, he decided to give up.

"Guess there's no use staying here here any longer," he remarked. "I'll push the thing and run for home."

He started down the road in the storm and darkness. The highway soon became a long puddle of mud, through which he splashed, finding it more and more difficult every minute to push the bicycle in the thick, sticky clay.

Tom was about to pick it up and shoulder the load when, above the roar of the wind and the swishing of the rain, he heard another sound. It was a steady "ch-puff ch-puff," and then the darkness was cut by a glare of light.

"An automobile," said Tom aloud. "Guess I'd better get out of the way."

He turned to one side, but the auto, instead of passing him when it got to the place where he was, pulled over and made a sudden stop.

"Want a ride?" asked the chauffeur, peering out from the side curtains which somewhat protected him from the storm. Tom saw that the car was a large, touring model. "Can I give you a lift?" went on the driver.

"Well, I've got my bicycle with me," explained the young inventor over the sound of the rain and the auto's engine. "My chain's broken, and I've got a mile to go."

"Jump up in back," invited the man. "Leave your ride here. It ought to be safe over behind those trees."

"Oh, I couldn't do that," said Tom. "I don't mind walking. I'm wet through now, and I can't get much wetter. I'm much obliged, though."

"Well, I'm sorry, but I can hardly take you and the bicycle, too," continued the chauffeur.

"Certainly not," added a voice from the tonneau of the car. "We can't have a muddy bicycle in here. Who is that person, Simpson?"

"It's a young man, sir," answered the driver.

"Is he acquainted with the area?" went on the voice from the rear of the car. "Ask him if he is acquainted with the area, Simpson."

Tom was wondering where he had heard that voice before. He had a vague notion that it was familiar.

"Are you acquainted with the around here?" obediently asked the man at the wheel.

"I live here," replied Tom. He found himself becoming slightly annoyed at the invisible questioner.

"Ask him if he knows any one named Swift?" continued the voice from the tonneau, and the driver started to repeat it.

"Do you—"

"I heard him," interrupted Tom. "Yes, I know a Mr. Swift," but Tom, with a sudden resolve, and one he could hardly explain, decided that for the present he would not reveal his own identity.

"Ask him if this Mr. Swift is an inventor." Once more the unseen person spoke in the voice Tom was trying vainly to recall.

The chauffeur looked pointedly at Tom.

"Yes, Mister Swift is an inventor," was the youth's answer.

"Do you know much about him? What are his habits? Does he live near his workshops? Does he confide in anyone regarding his work? Does he keep many servants? Does he—"

The unseen man suddenly parted the side curtains and peered out at Tom, who stood in the muddy road close to the automobile. At that moment there came a bright flash of lightning, illuminating not only Tom's face, but that of his questioner as well.

And at the sight of their momentarily-illuminated faces, Tom started no less than did the man. Tom recognized him as another one of the three mysterious persons in the restaurant.

As for the man, he had also recognized Tom.

"Ah—er—um—is—Why, it's you, isn't it?" said the questioner, and he thrust his head farther out from between the curtains. "My, what a storm!" he exclaimed as the rain increased. "So you know Mr. Swift, eh? I saw you today in Mansburg, I think. I have a good memory for faces. Do you work for Mr. Swift? If you do I may be able to make this worth—"

"I'm Tom Swift, son of Mr. Barton Swift," said Tom as quietly as he could.

"Tom Swift! His son!" cried the man, and he seemed even more agitated. "Why, I thought—that is, Morse said—Simpson, hurry back to Mansburg!" and with that, taking no more notice of Tom, the man in the auto hastily pulled his head back inside the auto and drew the curtains together.

The chauffeur threw the auto into gear and swung the ponderous machine to one side. The road was wide, and he required two attempts before finally getting aimed in the correct direction. He almost ended up with the front end in the opposite ditch but managed to stop and reverse in the nick of time.

A moment later the car was speeding back the way it had come, leaving Tom standing on the highway, alone and wet in the mud and darkness, with the rain pouring down in torrents.

TOM SWIFT and His Motorcycle

CHAPTER VII

OFF ON A SPIN

TOM'S FIRST IMPULSE was to run after the automobile, the red tail lights of which glowed through the blackness like retreating ruby eyes. Then he realized that it was going at such a pace that it would be impossible to get near it, even if his bicycle had been in working order.

Even if it had not been pouring rain.

"If I had my motorcycle I'd catch up to them," he murmured. Then he thought, "I must hurry home and tell dad. This is another link in the odd chain that seems to be winding around us. I wonder who that man was, and why he was asking so many personal questions about dad?"

Pushing his bicycle before him, with the chain dangling from the handlebar, Tom splashed on through the mud and rain. It was a lonesome, weary walk, tired as he was with the happenings of the day, and the young inventor breathed a sigh of thankfulness as the lights of his home shone out in the mist of the storm.

As he tramped up the steps of the side porch, his bicycle bumping along ahead of him, the door was thrown open.

"Goodness, Tom!" exclaimed Mrs. Baggert. "Look at the state of you. Whatever happened to you?" and she hurried forward in a kindly manner, for the housekeeper was almost a second mother to the youth.

"Chain broke," answered the lad laconically. "Where's dad?"

"Out in the shop, working at his latest invention, I expect. But are you hurt?"

"Oh, no, I just got caught short by a mile or thereabouts. The mud was soft as a feather-bed, you know, except that it isn't so good for the clothes," and the young inventor looked down at his splashed and bedraggled garments.

He knew that Mrs. Baggert would retrieve the soiled items from the hamper and have them washed before he arose the following morning, such was her habit.

Mr. Swift was very surprised and dismayed when Tom told him of the happening on the road, and the conversation—and the subsequent alarm—of the man on learning Tom's identity.

"Who do you suppose he could have been?" asked Tom, when he had finished.

"I am pretty certain he was one of that crowd of financiers of whom Amberson Morse seems to be a representative," said Mr. Swift. "It was his name n that telegram you found. Are you sure he was one of those you saw in the restaurant?"

"Positive. I had a good look at him both times. In fact, he mentioned someone called Morse when exclaiming his surprise. Something like, 'Morse said,' or the likes. Do you think he imagines he could come here and get possession of your secrets?"

"I hardly know what to think, Tom. But we will take every

precaution, especially now that Amberson Morse's name has come into it all. We will set all the burglar alarm wires tonight. I have neglected them for some time, as I fancied everything would be secure here. Then, I will take my plans and the model of the turbine motor into the house. I'll run no chances tonight."

Mr. Swift, who had been installing and adjusting some of the new bolts that Tom had brought home earlier, began to gather up his tools and materials.

"I'll help you, Dad," said Tom, and he began the process of connecting the burglar alarm wires. These were part of an elaborate system strung all about the house, shops and grounds. Anyone walking into one or simply touching it, set off an alarm that could be heard throughout the Swift house. Lights outside would come on and several well-positioned camera would be set off using a spring-loaded mechanism.

Neither Tom nor his father slept well that night. Several times one or the other of them arose, thinking they heard unusual noises. Usually, it was only some disturbance caused by the storm, and morning arrived without anything unusual having taken place. The rain still continued and Tom, looking out a window and seeing the downpour, remarked, "I'm glad of it!"

"Why?" asked his father, who was in the next room.

"Because I'll have a good excuse for staying in and working on my new motorcycle."

"But you had promised to do some studying," declared Mr. Swift. "You promised to recite your mathematics results right after breakfast."

"All right, Dad. I guess you'll find I've done my lessons."

Tom had graduated with honors from a local academy, and a full year ahead of others his age. When it came to a question of going further in his studies, he had elected to continue with his father as his tutor, instead of going directly to college. That would come later, when he had turned at least twenty years of age.

Mr. Swift was a very learned man, and this arrangement was satisfactory to him as it allowed Tom more time at home. He could both aid his father on the inventive work and also develop things for himself. Tom showed a taste and aptitude for mechanics and electrical studies, and his father wisely decided that such training as his son needed could be given at home to better advantage than in any nearby school or college.

Lessons over and satisfied with Tom's work, Barton Swift returned to his workshop and his work on completing the working model of his turbine.

Tom hurried to his own small shop and began taking apart the damaged motorcycle.

"First I'll straighten the handlebars and then see if there is any damage to the motor and transmission," he decided. "The new front wheel I can buy in town. This one is hardly worth repairing."

Tom was soon busy with wrenches, hammers, pliers and screw-driver. He was in his element, and was whistling over his task. As he suspected, once removed the handlebars required straightening in more than one direction. He quickly rigged a jig on his workbench and use both hand strength and a small pulley to ease the metal back into alignment.

While he had the metal tubes removed he decided to see about opening a set of small holes in the metal so that the control cables might be run on the inside, rather than flapping about on the outside, of the bars.

He soon had them rigged to his satisfaction and remounted the handlebars.

The motor he found in general good condition. Tom

believed from his observations of Mr. Damon that the motor made greater noise than it provided in actual momentive power. He sat in thought about what he might do to fix that.

"I planned to re-gear the transmission, which might provide some extra speed," he considered, "but the actual motor seems to lack overall power." He removed the magneto assembly which provided power to the single spark plug of the one-cylinder motor.

A quick check showed that it was woefully inadequate for the amount of spark Tom believed the motor and its sparking plug could and should handle.

Within the hour Tom had rewired the coil using many yards of thin copper wire he had on a spool. To protect it from weather and dampness, he carefully coated it in a thick layer of beeswax. Though ending up the same size and appearance, testing showed it to be almost half again as powerful as the original.

Tom was pleased with his results.

Next, he checked the spark plug. It turned the power coming from the magneto into a spark that set the gasoline and air mixture alight. As he suspected, the manufacturer had the spark gap set so that the motor provided minimal power. He took out his pliers and a small gauge and soon had reset the gap wider.

It was not such an easy task as he had hoped to change the transmission. He finally needed to ask his father's advice in order to get the right proportion between the back and front gears. The motorcycle was operated by a sprocket chain similar to his bicycle—though of heavier build—instead of a belt drive, as is the case with some motorcycles.

Mr. Swift showed Tom how to compute the number of teeth needed on each sprocket in order to get an increase of speed while not taxing the power of the motor. As there was a spare sprocket wheel of appropriate size from a disused piece of machinery available, Tom took that.

He soon had everything back in place, and then tried the motor. To his delight the number of revolutions of the rear wheel were increased about fifteen per cent at low settings. Tom could hardly wait to see what it would do at road speeds.

"I know I'll make better speed," he announced to his father. "It should go up hills better as well."

"But it will take more gasoline to run the motor, don't forget that. You know the great principle of mechanics—that you can't get out of a machine any more than you put into it, nor quite as much, as a matter of fact. You will lose considerable power through friction."

"Well, then, I'll make a larger gasoline tank," declared Tom. "I want to go fast when I'm going. And far as well."

He looked at the reassembled machine. After several hours of work it was practically in shape to run, except that a front wheel was lacking.

"I think I'll ride to town and get one," he remarked. "The rain isn't quite so hard now."

In spite of his father's mild objections, Tom went on his bicycle, the chain of which he quickly repaired. He found exactly the front wheel needed, and by that night his motorcycle was ready to run. But it was too dark to try it then, especially as he had no good lantern. The lantern and reflector and lens on the cycle had been smashed in the accident. And his own bicycle light was not powerful enough. So, he postponed his trial trip until the next day.

"I'll see about ordering a new lamp when I get to town."

He was up early the following morning, and went out for a test spin before breakfast. He came back, with flushed cheeks and bright eyes, just as Mr. Swift and Mrs. Baggert were sitting down to the table.

"To Reedville and back," announced Tom proudly.

"What? A round trip of thirty miles!" exclaimed Mr. Swift. "You only left forty minutes ago!"

"I know," declared his son. "I went like a greased pig most of the way. I had to slow up going through Mansburg, but the rest of at time I let it out for all it was worth."

"You must be careful," cautioned his father. "You are not an expert yet."

"No, I realize that. Several times when I wanted to slow up, I began to back-pedal, forgetting that I wasn't on my bicycle. Then I thought to shut off the power and put on the brake. But it's glorious fun. I'm going out again as soon as I have something to eat. That is, unless you want me to help you, Dad."

"No, not this morning. Learn to ride your motorcycle. It may come in handy."

Neither Tom nor his father realized what an important part the machine was soon to play in their lives.

Tom went out for another spin after breakfast, and in a different direction. He wanted to see what the machine would do on a hill, and there was a long, steep one about five miles from home. The roads were in fine shape after the rain, and he sped up the incline at a rapid rate.

"It certainly does eat up the road," the lad murmured. "I have improved this machine considerably. Wish I could take out a patent on it."

As he traveled along he noticed that he was having to rub specks of dust from his eyes frequently, and that his face became a target for the impact of small insects.

"I'm going to need to develop some sort of head gear to keep those things out of my eyes. Imagine what would happen if I had a wasp or something dangerous like that hit me in the eye while traveling a top speed. Whew!"

Reaching the crest of the slope, he started down the incline. He turned down part of the power, and was gliding along joyously, when from a cross-road he suddenly saw a mule turn into the main highway pulling ing a ramshackle wagon loaded with fence posts. Next to the animal walked an old colored man.

"I hope he gets out of the way in time," thought Tom. "He's moving as slow as molasses, and I'm going a bit faster than I like. Guess I'll shut down and put on the brakes."

The mule and wagon were now squarely across the road. Tom was coming nearer and nearer. He turned the handle-grip, controlling the supply of gasoline, and to his horror found that it was stuck. He could not stop the motorcycle!

"Look out! Look out!" cried Tom to the negro. "Get out of the way! I can't stop! Let me pass you!"

The black man looked up. He saw the approaching machine, and he seemed to freeze in place.

"Whoa, Boomerang!" cried the man. "Whoa! Somefin's gwine t' happen!"

"Please move," muttered Tom desperately, as he saw that there was no room for him to pass without going into the ditch, an event that would mean an upset or worse. "Pull out of the way!" he yelled again.

But either the driver could not understand, or did not appreciate the necessity. The mule stopped and reared up. The colored man hurried to the head of the animal to quiet it.

"Whoa, Boomerang! Jest yo' stand still!" he said.

Tom, with a great effort, managed to twist the grip and finally shut off the gasoline. But it was too late. In a skid he struck the black man with the front wheel. Fortunately Tom had managed to reduce his speed by a quick application of the brake, or the result might have been more serious.

As it was, the man was lifted away from the mule's head and tossed into the long grass next to the ditch. Tom, by a great effort, succeeded in maintaining his seat in the saddle, and then, bringing the machine to a stop, he leaped off and turned back.

The colored man was sitting up, looking dazed.

"Whoa, Boomerang!" he murmured. "Somefin's done happened!"

But the mule, who had quieted down, only waggled his ears lazily and let out a soft bray. Tom, ready to laugh now that he saw he had not committed manslaughter, hurried to where the colored man was sitting.

TOM SWIFT and His Motorcycle

―――

CHAPTER VIII

SUSPICIOUS ACTIONS

"ARE YOU HURT?" asked Tom as he leaned his motorcycle against the fence and stood beside the negro.

"Hurt?" repeated the black man. "I'se killed, dat's what I is! I ain't got a whole complete bone in mah body! Good golly, but I suttinly am in a awful state! Would yo' mind tellin' me if dat darn mule of mine is still alive?"

"Of course he is," answered Tom. "He isn't hurt a bit. Why don't you turn around and look for yourself?"

"No, sah! No, indeedy, young sah!" replied the colored man. "Yo' doan catch dis here haid lookin' around!"

"Why not?"

"Why not? 'Cause I'll tell yo' why not. I'm so stiff an' I'm so nearly broke t' pieces, dat if I turn mah head around it shuhly will twist offen mah body. No, sah! No, indeedy, sah, I ain't gwine t' turn 'round. But is yo' shuh dat mah mule Boomerang ain't hurted?"

"No, he's not hurt a bit, and I'm sure you are not. I never touched your mule, and I didn't strike you hard, since I had almost stopped my machine. Let me help you try to get up. I'm positive you'll find yourself all right. I'm really sorry it happened."

"Oh, dat's all right. Doan mind me," went on the colored man. "It was mah fault fer gittin in de road. But dat mule Boomerang is suttinly de most outrageous quadruped dat ever circumlocuted."

"Why do you call him Boomerang?" asked Tom, wondering if the negro man was really hurt.

"What fo' I call him Boomerang? Did you eber see dem Australian black mans what goes around with de circus and t'row dem crooked sticks dey calls boomerangs?"

"Yes, I've seen them."

"Well, Boomerang, mah mule, he's jest laik dat. He's crooked, t' begin wid, an' anudder t'ing, yo' can't never tell when yo' start him whar he's gwine t' land up. Dat's why I calls him Boomerang."

"I see. It's a very proper name. But why don't you try to get up?"

"Does yo' think I can?"

"Sure. Try it. By the way, what's your name?" Tom asked as the man slowly started to rise, then sat back down with a grunt.

"My name? Why I was christened Andrew Jackson Abraham Lincoln Sampson, but folks most gennally calls me Eradicate Sampson. Some doan't eben go to dat length. Dey jest calls me Rad, fo' short."

"Eradicate," mused Tom. "That's a odd name, too. Why are

you called that?"

"Well, yo' see I eradicates dirt. I'm a cleaner an' a whitewasher by profession, an' somebody gib me dat name. Dey said it were fitten an' proper, an' I kept it eber sence. Yes, sah. I'se Eradicate Sampson, an I'm at yo' service." He looked Tom up and down. "Yo' ain't got no chicken coops yo' wants cleaned out, has yo'? Or any stables or fences t' whitewash? I guarantees satisfaction."

"Well, I might find some work for you to do," replied the young inventor, thinking this would be as good a means as any of placating the black man. "But come, now, try and see if you can't stand. I don't believe I broke any of your legs."

"I guess not. I feels better now. Where might be dat work yo' was speakin' of?" and Eradicate Sampson, now that there seemed to be a prospect of earning money, rose quickly and easily, brushing off a bit of dust from where he had landed.

"See, you're all right!" exclaimed Tom, glad to find that the accident had had no serious consequences.

"Yes, sah, I guess I be. Whar did yo' say, yo' had some whitewashin' t' do?"

"No place in particular, but there is always something that needs doing at our house. If you call by later in the week I'll give you a job."

"Yes, sah, I'll be sure to call," and Eradicate walked back to where Boomerang was patiently waiting. He patted the mule affectionately and turned to Tom. "Whare is it yo' be libin?"

Tom told the colored man how to find the Swift home, and was debating with himself whether he ought not to offer Eradicate some money as compensation for knocking him into the air, when he noticed that the negro had begun tying one wheel of his wagon right to the body of the vehicle with a rope.

"What are you doing that for?" asked Tom.

"Got to, t' git downhill wid dis load of fence posts," was the answer. "If'n I didn't it would run up right on to de heels o' Boomerang, an' wheneber he feels anyt'ing on his heels he does act wuss dan a circus mule!"

"But why don't you use your brake? I see you have one on the wagon. Use the brake to hold back going downhill."

"'Scuse me, Mistah Swift, 'scuse me!" exclaimed Eradicate quickly. "But yo' doan know dat brake. It's wuss dan none at all. It doan work, fer a fact. No, indeedy, young sah. I'se got to rope de wheel."

Tom was interested at once. He made an examination of the brake, and soon saw why it would not hold the wheels. The foot lever was not properly connected with the brake bar. It was a simple matter to adjust it by changing a single bolt, and this Tom did with tools he took from the bag on his motorcycle.

The colored man looked on in open-mouthed amazement. Even Boomerang peered lazily around, as if taking an interest in the proceedings.

Tom noticed that the piece of leather strap that kept the wood of the brake and the wood of the axle from rubbing dangerously together was thin and weather worn. He had neither the leather strap nor the proper tools to install a new one.

"There," said Tom at length, as he tightened the nut. "That brake will work now, and hold the wagon on any hill. You won't need to rope the wheel. You simply didn't have the right leverage on it."

"'Scuse me, Mistah Swift, but what's dat yo' said?" and Eradicate leaned forward to listen deferentially.

"I said you didn't have the right leverage."

"No, sah, Mistah Swift, 'scuse me, but yo' made a slight mistake. I ain't never had no liverage on dis here wagon. It ain't dat kind of a wagon. I onct drove a livery rig, but dat were some years ago. I ain't worked fo' de livery stable in some time now. Dat's why I *know* dere ain't no livery on dis wagon. Yo'll 'scuse me, but yo' is slightly mistaken."

"All right," rejoined Tom with a laugh, not thinking it worth while to explain what he meant by the lever force of the brake rod. "Let it go at that. Livery or no livery, your brake will work now. I guess you're all right. Now don't forget to come around and do some whitewashing," and seeing that the colored man was able to mount to the seat and start off Boomerang, who seemed to have deep-rooted objections about moving, Tom wheeled his motorcycle back to the road.

Eradicate Sampson drove his wagon a short distance and then suddenly applied the brake. It stopped short, and the mule looked around as if surprised.

"It shuh do work, Mistah Swift!" called the black man to Tom, who was waiting the result of his little repair job. "It shuh do! I'm a thankin' yo mighty."

"I'm glad of it."

"Good golly! But yo's suttinly a conjure-man when it comes t' fixin' wagons! Did yo' eber work fer a blacksmith?"

"No, not exactly. Say. Remind me when you come to our home and I'll fit a new piece of leather on that brake so that you don't have the wood on wood start a fire. Well, goodbye, Eradicate. I'll look for you some day next week."

With that Tom leaped on his machine, set the spark and jumped on the starter handle. He speed off ahead of the colored man and his rig. As he passed the load of fence posts the youth heard Eradicate remark in awestricken tones, "Mah golly! He suttinly go laik de wind! An' t' think dat I were hit by dat monstrousness machine, an' not hurted! Mah golly!

T'ings is suttinly happenin'! G't long, Boomerang!"

"This machine has more possibilities in it than I suspected," mused Tom as man and mule disappeared behind him. "But one thing I've got to change, and that is the gasoline and spark controls. I don't like them the way they are. I want a better leverage with no sticking, just as Eradicate needed on his wagon. I'll fix them, too, when I get home."

He rode for several hours, until he thought it was about lunch time. Then, heading the machine toward home, he put on all the speed possible, soon arriving where his father was at work in the shop.

"Well, how goes it?" asked Mr. Swift with a smile as he looked at the flushed face of his son.

"Fine, Dad! I scooted along in great shape. Had an adventure, too."

"You didn't meet any more of those men, did you? The men who are trying to get my invention?" asked Mr. Swift apprehensively.

"No, Dad. I simply had a little run-in with a man named Eradicate Andrew Jackson Abraham Lincoln Sampson, otherwise known as Eradicate or Rad Sampson, and I engaged him to do some whitewashing for us. We do need some white washing done, don't we, Dad?"

"What's that?" asked Mr. Swift, thinking his son was joking.

Then Tom told of the slight accident.

"Yes, I think I can find some work for Eradicate to do," went on Mr. Swift once he knew the reasons. "There is some dirt in the boiler shop that needs, er, eradicating, and I think he can do it as well. But lunch has been waiting some time. We'll go in now, or Mrs. Baggert will be out after us."

Father and son were soon seated at the table, and Tom was explaining what he meant to do to improve his motorcycle.

His father offered some suggestions regarding the placing of the gasoline lever.

"I'd put it here," he said, and with his pencil he began to absently draw a diagram on the white table cloth. "That, plus you might think of building a new set of cables. Perhaps run the cable wires inside of greased rubber hoses. They shouldn't stick that way"

"Oh, my goodness me, Mr. Swift!" exclaimed Mrs. Baggert. "Whatever are you doing?" and she sprang up in some alarm.

"What's the matter? Did I upset my tea?" asked the inventor innocently looking around.

"No, but you are soiling a clean tablecloth. Pencil marks are so hard to get out. Take a piece of paper, please."

"Oh, is that all?" rejoined Mr. Swift with a smile. "Well, Tom, here is the way I would do that," and substituting the back of an envelope for the tablecloth, he continued the drawing.

Tom was looking over his father's shoulder when Mrs. Baggert, who was removing some of the dinner dishes, suddenly asked, "Are you expecting a visitor, Mr. Swift?"

"A visitor? No. Why?" asked the inventor quickly.

"Because I just saw a man going in the machine shop," went on the housekeeper.

"A man! In the machine shop!" exclaimed Tom, jumping from his chair. Mr. Swift hurriedly got up, and the two rushed from the house. As they reached the yard they saw a man emerging from the building where Mr. Swift was constructing his turbine motor. The man had his back turned toward them and seemed to be sneaking around, as though hoping to escape observation.

"What do you want?" called Mr. Swift angrily.

The man turned quickly. At the sight of Mr. Swift and Tom

he made a jump to one side and ran behind a big packing box.

Mr. Swift and Tom started on a run toward where the man was hiding, Tom following his father. As the two inventors reached the box, the man sprang from behind it and ran down the yard to a lane that passed in back of the Swift house. As he ran he was seen to stuff several papers in his pocket.

"My plans! He's stolen some of my plans!" cried Mr. Swift. "Catch him, Tom!"

Tom sprinted after the stranger while Mr. Swift entered the shop to ascertain whether anything had been stolen.

TOM SWIFT and His Motorcycle

―――

CHAPTER IX

A FRUITLESS PURSUIT

DOWN THROUGH the yard Tom speed in and out among the buildings looking on every side for a sight of the bold stranger. No one was to be seen.

"He can't be very far ahead." thought Tom. "I need to catch him before he gets to the woods. If he reaches there he has a good chance of getting away."

There was a little patch of trees just back of the inventor's house, not much of a woods perhaps, but that is what they were called.

"I wonder if he is one of the gang after dad's invention?" thought Tom as he sprinted ahead.

By this time he was clear of the group of buildings and in sight of a tall, board fence which surrounded the Swift estate on three sides. Here and there along the fence were piled enough old packing cases that it would be easy for the fugitive to leap atop one of them and get over the fence. Tom thought of this possibility in a moment.

"I guess he got over ahead of me," the lad exclaimed, and he peered sharply about. "I'll catch him on the other side!"

As he turned, Tom tripped over a plank and went down full length, making quite a racket. When he picked himself up he was surprised to see the man he was after dart from inside one of the empty boxes and start for the fence near a point where there were other packing cases piled up.

The man was making a fast approach to the barrier. Tom realized that the fugitive had been hiding, waiting for a chance to escape, and Tom's fall had alarmed him and forced his hand.

"Here! Hold on there! Come back!" cried the youth as he recovered his wind and leaped forward.

But the man did not stop. With a bound he was up on the pile of boxes, and the next moment he was poised on top of the fence. Before leaping down on the other side, a ten-foot jump even a practiced athlete might well hesitate to make, the fleeing stranger paused and looked back. Tom gazed at him and recognized the man in an instant. He was the third of the mysterious trio whom the lad had seen in the Mansburg restaurant.

"Wait a minute! You can't go sneaking around here," shouted Tom as he ran forward. The man spun around again and jumped. An instant later, he disappeared from view on the other side of the fence.

"He jumped down!" thought Tom. "A big leap, too. Well, I've got to follow. This is all so strange. First one, then the second, and now the third of those men seem determined to get something here. I hope this one didn't succeed. I'll soon find out."

He scrambled up the pile of packing cases and leapt over the fence, jarring himself. He straightened up and caught a glimpse of the fugitive running toward the woods, and took after the man.

While Tom was a good runner, he was handicapped by the fact that the man had a start of him, and also by the fact that the stranger had had a brief rest while hiding in the big box. So it is no great wonder that he quickly found himself being distanced.

Once, twice he called on the fleeing one to halt, but the man paid no attention, and did not even look around. Tom wisely concluded to save his wind for running. He did his best, but was chagrined to see the man reach the woods ahead of him.

"I've lost him now," thought Tom. "Well, there's no help for it."

Still he did not give up, and kept on through the patch of trees. On the far side lay Lake Carlopa, a broad and long sheet of water.

"If he doesn't realize that the lake's there," thought our hero, "he may keep straight on. The water will be sure to stop him, and then I can catch him along the shore. But what will I do with him after I get him? I guess I've got a right to demand to know what he was doing around our place, and what those papers he has are."

Tom could hear the fugitive ahead of him, and marked his progress by the crackling of the underbrush. The man seemed intent on escape, not confrontation, and took no pains to disguise the noises of his flight.

"Almost up to him," exulted the young inventor. Then, at the same moment, he caught sight of the man running and a glimpse of the sparkling water of Lake Carlopa. "Got him! I've got him!" Tom almost cried aloud in his excitement. "Unless he takes to the water and swims for it, I've got him!"

But Tom did not reckon on a very simple matter; that was the possibility of the man having a boat at hand. Which is what happened.

Reaching the lake shore the fugitive put on a final spurt of speed and managed to put a slightly greater distance between himself and Tom.

Drawn up on the beach was a little motorboat. After he had pushed it from shore, the stranger leaped in and grabbed the starter rope. It was the work of but a second to set the engine going and the boat in motion.

As Tom reached the edge of the woods and started across the narrow strip of sand and gravel that ran between the water and the trees, he saw the man steering his craft toward the middle of the lake. He was already fifty feet out.

"Well—I'll be jiggered!" exclaimed the youth, stopping and panting, hands on hips. "Who would have thought he'd have a motorboat waiting for him? This was obviously a well-planned theft."

There was nothing to do but turn back. Although Tom kept a small rowboat and a sailing skiff on the lake, his boathouse was some distance away. Even if he could get one of his craft out, the motorboat would soon distance it.

"He's gone!" thought the searcher regretfully. He looked out across the water.

The man in the motorboat did not look back. He sat low in the middle of his small boat, steering the little craft right across the broadest part of Lake Carlopa.

"I wonder where he came from, and where he's going?" mused Tom. "That's a boat I never saw on this lake before. It looked to be a new one. Well, there's no help for it, I've got to go back and tell dad I couldn't catch him."

And with a last look at the fugitive, who, with his boat, was becoming smaller and smaller every minute, Tom turned and retraced his steps.

TOM SWIFT and His Motorcycle

———

CHAPTER X

OFF TO ALBANY

"DID YOU CATCH him, Tom?" asked Mr. Swift eagerly when his son returned, but the inventor needed but a glance at the lad's despondent face to have his question answered without words, "Never mind," he added, "there's not much harm done, fortunately."

"Did he get anything? Any of your plans or models, Dad?"

"No, not as far as I can discover. Several stacks of my papers in the shop do not appear to have been disturbed, but it looked as if the turbine model was moved around. No damage. The only thing missing seems to be a few sheets of unimportant calculations. Mostly mathematical doodles for other projects. I believe he thought that they looked important. Luckily I have my most valuable drawings locked up in the safe in the house."

"That man seemed to be putting several papers in his pocket, Dad. Can you be certain he didn't steal any copies of your drawings."

"That's possible, Tom, and I admit it worries me. I can't imagine who that man is, unless—"

"He's one of the three men I saw in Mansburg in the restaurant," said Tom eagerly. "Two of them have tried to get information here, and now the third one comes. He got away in a motorboat," and Tom told how the fugitive escaped.

Mr. Swift looked worried. It was not the first time attempts had been made to steal his inventions, but on this occasion a desperate and well-organized plan appeared to be afoot.

"What do you think they are up to, Dad?" asked Tom.

"I still think they are trying to get hold of my turbine motor, Tom. You know I told you that the financiers were disappointed in the turbine they bought of another inventor. They were swindled as it does not work. To get back the money they spent, or to put it to some, possibly nefarious use, they must have a motor that is successful. Hence their efforts to get control of mine. I don't know whether I told you or not, but some time ago I refused a very good offer for certain rights in my invention. I knew it was worth more, especially to assist in any future war efforts. The offer came through Elrod & Drimble, the lawyers. When I refused it they seemed more than disappointed. More as if they were angry or even frightened of something. I think now that this same firm, and the financiers who have employed them, are trying by all the means in their power to get possession of my ideas, if not the invention and model itself."

"What can you do, Dad? You don't think they might be after you as well, do you?"

"Well, I must think. I certainly have to take some means to protect myself. I should have locked the workshop before going into he house. I did not think those men would be so unscrupulous or come back so soon."

"Do you know their names?"

"No, only from that telegram we found, the one which the first stranger dropped. One of them must be Amberson Morse. Who the others are, I don't know. But now I must make plans to foil them. I may have to call on you for help, Tom."

"And I'll be ready any time you call on me, Dad," responded Tom, drawing himself up. "Can I do anything for you right away?"

"No, I must think of a plan."

"Then I am going to take the time to change my motorcycle a bit. I'll put some more improvements on it."

"And I will write some letters to my lawyers in Washington and ask their advice. I think I'll need you to take another telegram to town for me later. I need to urge the government to get involved or they might end up facing an enemy with destructive devices powered by my own turbine. Oh, how I dread having that happen!"

It took Tom the remainder of that day, and part of the next, to arrange the gasoline and spark control of his machine to his satisfaction. In the middle of which he rode his bicycle back to the small Shopton telegraph office and sent off Mr. Swift's plea to the Federal agents.

He ended up making two new levers and some connecting rods. This he did in his own machine shop, which was fitted up with a lathe and other apparatus. The lathe was run by power coming from a small engine, which was operated by an engineer, an elderly man to whom Mr. Swift had given employment for many years. He was Garret Jackson, and he kept so close to his engine and boiler-room that he was seldom seen outside of it except when the day's work was done.

The next afternoon Tom went out for a spin on his motorcycle. He found that the machine worked much better, and was easier to control. One of the levers provided better and immediate control over the amount of gasoline being sent to the motor, while the other one could be used to advance or retard the spark. He rode about fifteen miles away from home, and then returned.

As he entered the yard he saw, standing in the drive, a ramshackle old wagon drawn by a big mule which seemed to be asleep.

"I'll wager that's Boomerang," said Tom aloud, and the mule opened its eyes, wiggled its ears and took a step forward.

"Whoa dar, Boomerang!" exclaimed a voice, and Eradicate Sampson hurried around the corner of the house. "Dat's jest lake yo'," went on the colored man. "Movin' when yo' ain't wanted to." Then, as he caught sight of Tom, he exclaimed, "Why, if it ain't young Mistah Swift! Good golly! But dat livery brake yo' done fixed on mah wagon suttinly is fine. Ah kin go down de steepest hill widout ropin' de wheel."

"Glad of it," replied Tom. "Did you come to do some work?"

"Yes, sah, I done did. I found I had some time t' spahr, an' thinks ta myself dere might be some whitewashin' I could do hereabouts. Yo' see, I lib only 'bout two mile from here."

"Well, I guess you can do a few jobs," said Tom. "Wait here."

He hunted up his father, and obtained permission to set Eradicate at work cleaning out the chicken house and whitewashing it. The black man was soon at work. A little later Tom saw him putting on a thick coat of whitewash. Eradicate stopped at the sight of Tom, and made some curious arm motions.

"What's the matter, Rad?" asked the young inventor walking over to admire the man's good work.

"Nuttin'. It's jest that the whitewash done persist in runnin' down de brush handle an' inter mah sleeve. I'm soakin' wet from it now, an' I has t' stop ebery onct in a while 'coz mah sleeve gits full."

Tom saw what the trouble was. The white fluid did run down the long brush handle in a small rivulet. Tom had once seen a little rubber device on a window-cleaning brush that worked well, and he decided to try it for Eradicate.

"Wait a minute," Tom advised. "I think I can stop that for you."

The colored man was very willing to take a rest, but it did not last long, for Tom was soon back at the chicken coop. He had a wide rubber disk with a hole in the center the size of the brush handle. Slipping the disk over the wood, he pushed it about half way along, and then, handing the brush back to the man, told him to try it that way.

"Did yo' done put a charm on mah brush?" asked Eradicate somewhat doubtfully. "Some sort o' dat voo deroo stuff?"

"Yes, but more like a sort of hoodoo charm. Try it now."

The black man dipped his brush in the pail of whitewash, and then began to spread it on the sides of the coop near the top. The surplus fluid started to run down the handle, but, meeting the piece of rubber, came no farther. It did not run down the sleeve of Eradicate.

"Now, when you put the brush back in to get more whitewash that extra all just runs into the bucket," Tom explained.

"Well, I d'clar t' goodness! That suttinly is a mighty fine charm!" cried the colored man. "Yo' shuh is a perty nice gen'lman, all right. Now I kin work widout stoppin' t' empty mah sleeve of dat sticky stuff ebery minute. I'se suttinly obliged t' ya'."

"You're welcome, I'm sure," replied Tom. "I think some day I'll invent a machine for whitewashing, and then—"

"Doan do dat! Doan do dat!" begged Eradicate earnestly. "Dis, an' makin' dirt disappear, is de only perfessions I got. Doan go 'ventin' no machine, Mistah Swift. Not whilst I'se still a'breathin' an all. Or gits me some money an' kin retire ta luxtury."

"All right. I'll wait until you get rich."

"Ha, ha! Den yo' gwine t' wait a pow'ful long time," chuckled Eradicate as he went on with his whitewashing.

Tom entered his workshop and found a disused leather strap. Good to his word, punched a few holes into it and went back out and replaced the worn leather on Eradicate's wagon with the new piece. Boomerang lost interest in the procedure about half way through.

When he finished the task, Tom went into the house. He found his father busy with some papers at his desk.

"Ah, it's you, is it, Tom?" asked the inventor, looking up. "I was just hoping you would come in."

"What for, Dad?"

"Well, I have quite an important mission for you. I want you to go on a journey."

"A journey? Where?"

"To Albany. You see, I've been thinking over matters, and I have been in correspondence with my lawyers in regard to finalizing the rights to my turbine motor. I must take measures to protect myself. You know I have not yet taken out a complete patent on the machine. I have not done so because I did not want to put my model on exhibition in Washington. I don't want that, and the Navy folks don't want that as well. I was afraid some of those unscrupulous men would take advantage of me. The government is afraid that foreign spies would take photos or detailed notes and be able to reproduce it for their own means."

Tom nodded soberly. He knew that his father was under a great deal of pressure regarding this new turbine.

"Another point was that I had not perfected a certain governing device that goes on the motor. It keeps the thing from operating at too high a speed, something that could lead to an explosion. It would never do. That matter is now resolved, and I am ready to send my model to Washington, and take out the complete patent."

"But I thought you said you wanted me to go to Albany."

"So I do. I will explain. I have just had a letter from Reid & Crawford, my Washington attorneys. Mr. Crawford, the junior member of the firm, will be in Albany this week on some legal business. He agrees to receive my model and some papers there, and personally transport them back to Washington with him. In this way they will be well protected. You see, I have to be on my guard, and if I send the model to Albany instead of the national capital I may throw the plotters off the track. I feel that they are watching every move I make. As soon as you or I might start for Washington they would be on our trail. But you can go to Albany unsuspected. Mr. Crawford will wait for you there. I want you to start day after tomorrow."

"All right, Dad. I can start now, if you say so."

"No, there is no special need for haste. I have some matters to arrange. You might go to the station and inquire about trains to the State capital."

"Am I going by train?"

"Certainly. How else could you go?"

There was a look of excitement in Tom's eyes. He had a sudden idea.

"Dad," he exclaimed, "why couldn't I go on my motorcycle?"

"Your motorcycle?"

"Yes. I could easily make the trip on it in one day. The roads are good, and I would enjoy it. I can carry the model in back of me, tied down to the saddle. It is not very large and the weight wouldn't impact my steering or balance."

"Well," said Mr. Swift slowly, for the idea had not occurred to him, "I suppose that part would be all right. But you have not had much experience riding a motorcycle. Besides, you don't know the roads."

"I can inquire. Will you let me go, Dad?"

Mr. Swift appeared to hesitate.

"It will be fine!" went on Tom. "I would enjoy the trip, and there's another thing. If we want to keep this matter secret, the best plan would be to let me go on my machine. If those men are on the watch, they will not think that I have the model. They will think I'm just going for a pleasure jaunt. We could disguise the model."

Barton Swift considered the matter. His model was only about eighteen inches long and under six inches across. It might, he believed, be possible to hide in inside of a large rucksack that Tom could wear on his back.

"There's something in that," admitted Mr. Swift. Tom, seeing that his father was favorably inclined, renewed his arguments until the inventor finally agreed.

"It will be a great trip!" exclaimed Tom. "I'll go all over my machine now, to ensure that it's in good shape. You get your papers and model ready, Dad, and I'll take them to Albany for you. The motorcycle will come in handy."

Had Tom only known the dangers ahead of him, and the risks he was to run, he would not have whistled so light heartedly as he went over every nut and bolt on his machine.

Beginning that very evening Tom set to making sure his motorcycle was in top condition. He drained the oil from the motor's sump, filtered it three times to remove the normal impurities that built up, and even thoroughly washed the metal filter.

Returning the oil to the crankcase and topping it up with fresh oil from a barrel the Swifts kept on hand, he next checked all of the electrical connections. Finally, he checked the condition of the new levers.

He discovered than one of them, the one for spark adjustment, had become slightly bent. "I imagine I set the motorcycle up against the fence and right on that lever," he said to nobody but himself. "I'll need to devise some manner so that the motorcycle can be stood up without anything to lean against."

Tom thought for a moment on how he might go about this, but shrugged and put it to the back of his mind.

The next morning Tom arose and went straight to his workshop. Mrs. Baggert was displeased to see him rush out the door without any breakfast, but Tom told her he would be back in within the hour.

Tom dug through an old steamer trunk in the corner and soon came up with the object of his search.

On a vacation to see relatives in the midwest, Ned Newton had been given a leather football helmet by an uncle. That uncle had, in return, been given the helmet as a joke when he had mentioned that he had wanted to play in college but his mother would not allow it.

Ned had given it to Tom as a memento. Now, he had a use for it.

Tom pulled down several volumes of science and chemistry.

He wanted to devise something to coat the helmet with so that it might better withstand any accident.

In a very short time he found several possibilities. The most promising being a blend of natural rubber, gutta-percha—a plant sap—and cellulose all dissolved in a solvent. Finding what he required both in his workshop and in one of the storage sheds his father kept, Tom set to making his polymer concoction.

As soon as it was prepared, Tom applied coats inside and out to the helmet. In moments, the solvent had evaporated and the helmet now had a thin but solid shell. He checked a few notes and then began applying additional coats to the outside at thirty-minute intervals.

After the fourth coat, Tom stopped. He would allow the helmet to harden completely over the rest of the day then check its strength.

Mrs. Baggert was none to happy when he finally came back into the house.

"Tom," she said sternly but kindly. "You said you would be back in, and I will quote you one this, 'in less than an hour' to have your breakfast. It is now well past two in the afternoon!"

Tom apologized to the housekeeper.

"Now," she announced. "You sit right down and I'll make you a fine liver sandwich. Best thing for a growing boy. Liver and onions."

Tom gulped. Then, an inspiration came to him., "Gee, Mrs. Baggert. I wish I could stay but I must ride into Shopton to make a special purchase for the trip I will take for dad tomorrow. I need to get to the shops before they close. See you at dinner," he said as he quickly exited the kitchen and the house.

Tom only used that as an excuse to take his motorcycle out

on the road for a couple hours. He also used it to test his new reinforced helmet.

Within minutes he concluded that air holes would need to be drilled in several locations. By the time he had traveled just five miles, Tom's head was soaked in sweat.

That evening, the polymer coating proved to be brittle and the helmet suffered several breaks as Tom tried drilling the ventilation holes. This surprised him since as a whole piece, the helmet had been able to withstand many blows with a leather-clad hammer. It was only upon being pierced that it seemed to lose strength.

He would have to try again following his forthcoming trip. "Perhaps, if I drilled the holes first and then applied the coating."

The following day, the valuable model had been wrapped in water-proof paper and placed into Tom's backpack. A hidden lock would deter most attempts to open the bag quickly and a wire mesh surrounding the package would require metal cutters to get inside of.

Tom carefully pinned the papers which were to be handed to Mr. Crawford in an inside jacket pocket. They, too, would be safe from casual removal or discovery.

He was to meet the lawyer at a hotel in Albany.

"Now take care of yourself, Tom," cautioned his father as he bade him goodbye. "Don't try to make speed, as there is no special rush. I don't want you calling attention to yourself. Do you understand? And, above all, don't lose anything."

Tom lowered the automobile driving goggles he had decided to wear over his eyes, and said, "I'll won't, Dad," and with a wave of his hand to Mr. Swift and the housekeeper, who stood in the door to see him off, Tom jumped into the saddle and turned on the gasoline and set the spark lever.

With normal start up rattles and bangs, which were quickly subdued by the muffler, the machine gathered speed. In a moment it had disappeared down the road.

Tom was off for Albany.

TOM SWIFT and His Motorcycle

———

CHAPTER XI

A VINDICTIVE TRAMP

THOUGH BARTON Swift had told his son there was no necessity for any great speed, the young inventor could not resist the opportunity for pushing his machine to the limit. The road was a level one and in good condition, so the motorcycle fairly flew along. The day was pleasant, a warm sun shining overhead, and it was evident that early summer was crowding spring rather closely.

"This is glorious!" exclaimed Tom as he spun along. "I'm glad I dad let me take this trip. It was a great idea. Wish Ned Newton was along, though. He'd be great company for me. But, as Ned would say, there are two good reasons why he can't come. One is he has to work in the bank, and the other is that he has no motorcycle."

Tom swept past house after house along the road, heading in the opposite direction from the town of Shopton and the city of Mansburg. For several miles Tom's route took him through a country district. The first large town he would reach would be Thessaly.

He planned to get lunch there, but he had brought a few sandwiches with him to eat along the road in case he became hungry before he reached the place.

"I hope the package containing the model doesn't jar around too much," mused the lad as he reached behind to make sure that the precious bundle was safe inside his backpack. "Dad would be in a bad way if that should disappear. And the papers, too."

He put his hand to his inner pocket to feel that they were secure.

Coming to a little down-grade, Tom backed off some of the power, the new levers he had arranged to control the gasoline and spark working very well.

"I think I'll take the old wood road and pass through Glens Falls," Tom decided, after covering another mile or two. He was approaching a division in the highway. "It's a bit sandy," he went on, "and the going will be heavy, but it will be a good chance to test my machine. Besides, I'll save five miles, and, while I don't have to hurry, I may need time on the other end. I'd rather arrive in Albany a little before dusk than after dark. I can deliver the model and papers and have a good night's sleep before starting back. So the old wood road it will be."

The wood road was a seldom-used highway, which originally was laid out for just what the name indicated: to bring wood from the forest. With the logging of most of the trees long complete, the road became more used for ordinary traffic between the towns of Lake George and Glens Falls. But when the State built a new highway connecting these two places the old road fell into disuse, though it was several miles shorter than the new turnpike.

Tom thought that he would modify his route home so as to pass along the new highway running north from Albany. He knew that the road between Lake George and the state's capitol city had recently been covered in the new tarmacadam, a mixture of small rocks and tar that was rolled out into a smooth, hard, black ribbon of roadway. With no dips, holes, stones or dust, Tom would be able to take the motorcycle to top speed.

Tom began wondering if he had been foolhardy in not taking the new road on his trip south to deliver his precious cargo. He could have made up the extra distance by being able to drive faster on the newer road.

"Oh, well," he thought.

He turned off from the main thoroughfare, and was soon spinning along the sandy stretch which was shaded with trees that, in some places. met overhead forming a leafy arch. It was cool and pleasant, and Tom liked it.

"It isn't as bad as I thought," he remarked looking a the sun-dappled road ahead. "The sand is pretty thick, but this machine of mine appears to be able to maneuver through it."

Indeed, the motorcycle was doing remarkably well, but Tom found that he had to turn on full power, otherwise the big rubber wheels went deep into the soft soil. Along Tom rode, picking out the firmest places in the road. He was so intent on this that he did not pay much attention to what was immediately ahead of him, knowing that he was not very likely to meet other vehicles or pedestrians.

He was considerably startled therefore when, as he went around a corner where the bushes grew thick right down to the edge of the road, to see a figure emerge from the underbrush and start across his path. So quickly did the man appear that Tom was almost upon him in an instant. Even though the young inventor shut off the power and applied the brake, the front wheel bumped the man and knocked him down.

"Blimey! What's the matter with you? What are you trying to do—kill me? Why don't you ring a bell or blow a horn when you're coming?" The man sprung up from the soft sand where the wheel from the motorcycle had sent him and faced Tom angrily. Then Tom, who had quickly dismounted, saw that his victim was a ragged tramp.

"I'm sorry," began Tom. "You came out of the bushes so quickly that I didn't have a chance to warn you. And you didn't look. Did I hurt you much?"

"Well, youse might have. 'Tain't your fault dat youse didn't," and the tramp began to brush the dirt from his ragged coat. Tom was instantly struck by a curious fact. The tramp now used language more in keeping with his character, whereas, in his first surprise and anger, he had spoken in a more refined manner.

"Youse fellers ain't got no right t' ride dem machines like lightnin' along dees roads," the ragged man went on clinging to the use of words and expressions current among his supposed fraternity. Tom wondered about it, and then, ascribing the use of the better language to the fright caused by being hit by the machine, he thought no more about it at the time. He should have.

"I'm very sorry," went on Tom. "I'm assure you I didn't mean to. You see, I was going quite slowly, and—"

"You call dat slow, when youse hit me an' knocked me down?" demanded the tramp. "I'd oughter have youse arrested, dat's what, an' I would if dere was a cop handy."

"I wasn't going at all fast," said Tom, a little nettled that his conciliatory words should be so rudely received. "If I had been going full speed I'd have knocked you fifty feet. And, you wouldn't be up and grousing at me right now. I told you I as sorry."

"It's a good thing. Cracky—erm—den I'm glad dat youse wasn't goin' like dat," and the tramp seemed somewhat confused.

This time Tom looked at him more closely, for the change in his language had been very plain. The fellow seemed uneasy, and turned his face away. As he did so Tom caught a glimpse of what he was sure was the side of a false beard. It was altogether too well-kept a beard to be a natural one for such a dirty tramp, and it appeared to have pulled away from his jaw slightly.

"That fellow's disguised!" Tom thought. "He's playing a part. I wonder if I'd better take chances and spring it on him that I'm on to his game?"

Then the ragged man spoke again. "I suppose it was part my fault, cully. I didn't know dat any guy was comin' along on one of dem buzz-machines, or I'd been more careful. I don't suppose youse meant to upset me, did ya?" and he looked at Tom more boldly. This time his words seemed to come naturally, and his beard, now that Tom took a second look at it, looked so much a part of himself that the young inventor wondered if he could have been mistaken in his first surmise.

"Perhaps he was once a gentleman who turned tramp because of hard luck," thought Tom. "That would account for him using good language at times. Guess I'd better keep still." To the tramp he said, "I'm sure you realize that I didn't mean to hit you. I admit I never expected to meet any one on this road. I certainly didn't expect to see a—"

He paused in some confusion. He was about to use the term "tramp," and he hesitated, not knowing how it would be received by his victim.

"Oh, dat's all right, cully. Call me a tramp, a vagabond bindlestiff. I know dat's what youse was goin' t' say. I'm used t' it. I've been a hobo so many years now dat I don't mind. De time was when I was a decent chap, though. But I'm a tramp now. Say, youse couldn't lend me a quarter, could youse?"

He approached closer to Tom, and looked quickly up and down the road. The highway was deserted, nor was there any likelihood that any one would come along. Tom was apprehensive, for the tramp was a burly man. The young inventor, however, was not so much alarmed at the prospect of a personal encounter, as that he feared he might be robbed, not only of his money but the valuable papers and model he carried. Even if the tramp was content with merely taking his money, it would mean that Tom would have to go back home for more, and that would delay his trip.

It was with no little alarm that he watched the ragged man coming closer. An idea came into Tom's head. He quickly shifted his position and brought the motorcycle between the man and himself. He resolved that if the tramp showed a disposition to attack him, he could push the machine over on him, and this would give Tom a chance to attack the thief to better advantage. However, the "hobo" showed no evidence of wanting to resort to highwayman methods. He paused a short distance from the machine, and said admiringly:

"Dat's a pretty shebang youse has."

"Yes, it's very fair," admitted Tom, who was not yet breathing easily.

"Kin youse go far on it?"

"Two hundred miles a day, easily."

"Fer cats' sake! An' I can't make half dat ridin' on de rails 'cause I gits put off so much. But say, is youse goin' to let me have dat quarter? I need it, honest I do. I ain't had nuttin' t' eat in two days."

The man's tone was whining. Surely he seemed like a genuine tramp, and Tom felt a little sorry for him. Besides, he felt that he owed him something for the unceremonious manner in which he had knocked the fellow down. Tom reached his hand in his pocket for some change, taking care to keep the machine between himself and the tramp.

"Are youse goin' far on dat rig-a-ma-jig?" went on the man

as he looked carefully over the motorcycle.

"Albany," answered Tom, and the moment the words were out of his mouth he wished he could recall them. All his suspicions regarding the tramp came back to him. But the ragged chap appeared to attach no significance to them.

"Albany? Dat's in Jersey, ain't it?" he asked.

"No, it's in New York," replied Tom, and then, to change the subject, he pulled out a half-dollar and handed it to the man. As he did so Tom noticed that the tramp had a tattoo on the little finger of his left hand of a blue ring.

"Dat's de stuff! Youse is a reg'lar millionaire, youse is!" exclaimed the tramp, and his manner seemed in earnest. "I'll remember youse, I will. What's your name, anyhow, cully?"

"Tom Swift," replied our hero, and again he wished he could bite back the truth. This time he was sure the tramp started and glanced at him quickly, but perhaps it was only his imagination.

"Tom Swift," repeated the man several times, and his tones were different from the whining ones in which he had asked for money. Then, as if recollecting the part he was playing, he added: "I suppose dey calls youse dat because youse rides so quick on dat machine. Har-har. But I'm sointainly obliged to youse—Tom Swift, an' I hopes youse gits t' Albany, in Jersey, in good time."

He turned away, and Tom was beginning to breathe more easily when the man spun and reached out and grabbed hold of the motorcycle. He gave it such a pull that it was torn from Tom's grasp which pulled him over and onto the ground. The lad was so startled at the sudden exhibition of vindictiveness an the part of the tramp that he did not know what to do. Then, before he could recover himself, the tramp pushed the motorcycle over and darted off into the bushes.

"I guess Happy Harry—dat's me—has spoiled your ride t'

Albany. Ha!" the tramp called as he escaped. "Maybe next time youse won't run down poor fellers on de road," and with that, the ragged man was lost to sight in the underbrush.

"Well, if that doesn't just say it all," mused Tom as he got back to his feet. "He must be crazy. I sure hope I don't meet you again, Happy Harry, or whatever your name is. Guess I'll get out of this neighborhood."

TOM SWIFT and His Motorcycle

CHAPTER XII

THREE MEN AND AN AUTO

TOM BEGAN by making sure that the package containing the model was still safely in place in his pack. He took the bag off his back and retrieved the key he had secreted in his shoe. Opening the bag, he felt around to make sure the model was still in one piece. Finding it seemed to be in fine condition he resealed the pack. He next put his hand in his pocket to see that he had the papers.

"They're all right," spoke Tom aloud. "I didn't know but what that chap might have worked a pickpocket game on me as I stumbled forward. I'm glad I didn't meet him after dark. Well, it's a good thing it's no worse. I wonder if he was trying to get my machine away from me or he is just vindictive? I doubt he'd know how to ride it if he did try to steal it."

Tom wheeled his motorcycle to a hard side-path along the old road and jumped into the saddle. He turned on the gasoline and spark and then pushed hard down on the starter lever to set the motor in motion. Nothing. He adjusted fuel and spark the levers and was dismayed that no explosion followed his second try. The motor seemed "dead."

"Oh. no," he thought, and tried starting the motor a third time. "It always starts easily. Maybe it doesn't like this sandy road."

It was hard work pushing the heavy machine along by "leg power," but, when he had acquired what he thought was sufficient speed, Tom turned on the power and hopped into the saddle while shifting it into gear. No explosions followed, and in some alarm he jumped back to the ground.

"Something's definitely wrong," he said aloud. "That tramp must have damaged the machine when he yanked it so and let it drop." Tom went quickly over the different parts. It did not take him long to discover what the trouble was. One of the wires, one leading from the battery to the magneto, which served to carry the current of electricity that exploded the mixture of air and gasoline, was missing. It had been broken off close to the battery box and the magneto.

"That's what Happy Harry did!" exclaimed Tom. "He pulled that wire off when he yanked my machine. That's what he meant by hoping I'd get to Albany. He was no tramp. He's disguised and up to some game. And he knows something about motorcycles, too, or he never would have taken that wire. I'm stalled, now; I haven't got another piece. I never thought to bring a replacement wire. I'll have to push this machine until I get to town, or else go back home."

The young inventor looked up and down the lonely road, undecided what to do. To return home meant that he would be delayed in getting to Albany, since he would lose a full day. If he pushed on to Glens Falls he might be able to get a bit of wire there.

Tom decided that was his best plan, and plodded on through the thick sand. He had not gone more than a quarter of a mile, each step seeming harder than the preceding one, when he heard a gun shot from the woods close to his left. He jumped and nearly let the motorcycle fall over.

For a split second the wild idea came into his head that the tramp had shot at him. With a quickly-beating heart Tom looked around. He could see nothing.

"I wonder if that was Happy Harry?" he mused. He pushed the machine over to a tree and leaned it against the trunk as quietly as he could. Crouching, he listened.

There was a crackling in the bushes and Tom, wondering what he might do to protect himself, looked toward the source of the noise.

A moment later a tall hunter stepped into view. The man carried a gun and wore a canvas suit. A belt about his waist was filled with cartridges.

"Oh. Hello!" he exclaimed pleasantly, Then, seeing a look of alarm on the lad's face, he went on, "I hope I didn't shoot in your direction, young man. Did I?"

"No—no, sir," replied the youthful inventor, who had hardly recovered his composure. "I heard your gun, and I imagined —"

"Gosh. Did you think you had been shot? Or, shot at? You must have a very vivid imagination. I fired in the air, but you couldn't have known that," he said muttering the last part almost to himself

"No, I didn't exactly think that," replied Tom, "but I just had an encounter with an ugly tramp, and I feared he might be using me for a target." He related an abbreviated tale of his encounter and of the damage to his motorcycle.

"Is that so. I hadn't noticed any tramps around here, and I've been in these woods nearly all day. Now that I think of it, I don't believe I've *ever* seen any tramps in these woods. Did he harm you?"

"No, not me. Only my motorcycle," and the lad explained.

"Gosh! That's too bad!" exclaimed the hunter. "I wish I could supply you with a bit of wire, but I haven't any. I'm just walking about, trying out my new gun."

"I shouldn't think you'd find much of anything to shoot this time of year," remarked Tom.

"Well, I don't expect to," answered the hunter, who had introduced himself as Theodore Duncan. "I have just purchased this fine new gun, and I wanted to try it. I expect to do considerable hunting this fall, and so I'm getting ready for it."

"Do you live near here?"

"About ten miles away, on the other side of Lake Carlopa, but I am fond of long walks in the woods. If you ever get to Waterford I invite you to come and see me, Mr. Swift. I have heard of your father."

"I will, Mr. Duncan, but if I don't get something to repair my machine with I'm not likely to get anywhere right away."

"Well, I wish I could help you, but I haven't the least bit of ingenuity when it comes to machinery. Now if I could help you track down that tramp—" He looked meaningfully at his gun.

"Oh, no, thank you. I'd rather not have anything more to do with him."

"If I caught sight of him now," resumed the hunter, "I fancy I could make him stop. Perhaps even give you back the wire. I'm a pretty good shot, even if this is a new gun. I've been practicing at improvised targets all day."

"No, the less I have to do with him, the better I'll like it," answered Tom, "though I'm much obliged to you. I'll manage somehow until I get to Glens Falls."

He started off again, the hunter disappearing in the woods. Presently, the sound of his gun was again heard.

"He's a bit of an odd man," murmured Tom, "but I like him. Perhaps I may see him when I go to Waterford, if I ever do."

Tom was destined to see the hunter again, at no distant time, and under strange circumstances.

But now the lad's whole attention was taken up with the difficulty in which he found himself. In vain, Tom mused on what purpose the tramp could have had in breaking off the wire. He trudged on.

"He might be one of the gang after dad's invention," thought Tom, "and he must have wanted to hinder me from getting to Albany, though why I can't imagine." With a dubious shake of his head Tom proceeded. It was hard work pushing the heavy machine through the sand, and he was puffing before he had gone very far.

Tom leaned the cycle against a nearby fence post and sat down to rest.

"I certainly am up against it," he murmured. "But if I can get a bit of wire in Glens Falls I'll be all right. If I can't—"

Just then Tom looked around him, and right at the fence. He spotted something which caused him to utter an exclamation of delight.

"That's the very thing!" he cried. "Why didn't I think of it before?"

Leaving his motorcycle standing against the post, Tom hurriedly looked over a wide section of the fence. The fence was a barbed-wire one, and in a moment Tom had found a broken strand of more that twenty inches.

"Guess no one will care if I take a piece of this," he reasoned. "It will have to do until I can get a real wire. I'll have it in place in a jiffy!"

It did not take long to get his pliers from his tool bag and snip off the piece of wire. Untwisting the double strands, he took out the sharp barbs, and then was ready to attach it to the binding posts of the battery box and the magneto.

"Hold on, though!" he exclaimed as he paused in the work. "It's got to be insulated, or it will vibrate against the metal of the machine and short circuit. I have it! My handkerchief! I suppose Mrs. Baggert will scold me for tearing up a good one, but I can't help it."

Tom took a spare handkerchief from the bundle in which he had a few belongings, carried with the idea of spending the night at an Albany hotel, and he was soon wrapping strips of linen around the wire and tying them with pieces of string.

"There!" he exclaimed at length. "That's insulated well enough, I guess. Now to fasten it on and start."

The young inventor, quick with his tools, soon had the improvised wire in place. He tested the spark and found that it was almost as good as the regular copper conductor. Then, having taken a spare bit of the barbed-wire along in case of another emergency, he jumped on the motorcycle and turned on the power.

"That's the stuff!" he cried as the welcome explosions sounded. "I guess I've fooled Happy Harry! I'll get to Albany pretty nearly on time, anyhow." But the tramp had Tom worried for quite a while.

He rode into Glens Falls, and asked a local policeman for some directions. In the local plumbing shop he located and purchased a length of insulated copper wire that would perform better than did the galvanized piece from the fence and almost as good as the original wire.

It was as he began attaching the new wire to the magneto that Tom noticed the sparking device had been slightly damaged as well. He spent another ten cents and bought both some thin copper wire and a candle. In less that ten minutes he had the magneto rewired and insulated with wax.

The reattachment was quickly made, and he was on his way

again. As it was getting close to noon he stopped near a little spring outside of Glens Falls and ate a sandwich, washing it down with the cold water. Then he started for Thessaly.

As he was coming into the small city he heard an automobile behind him. He steered to one side of the road and stopped to give the big car plenty of room to pass. It did not come on as speedily as he thought it would. He looked back and saw that it was going to stop near him. He shut off the power to his machine.

"Is this the road to Thessaly?" asked one of the trio of travelers in the auto. Tom could not discern their faces as all wore driving goggles and scarves wrapped around their lower faces.

"Straight ahead," answered the lad, an uneasy feeling creeping into his stomach.

At the sound of his voice one of the men in the big touring car leaned forward and whispered something to another in the front seat. The second man nodded, and looked closely at Tom. The youth, in turn, stared at the men. He still could not distinguish their faces.

"How many miles is it?" asked the man who had whispered, and at the sound of his voice Tom felt a vague sense that he had heard it before.

"Less than one," answered the young inventor, and once more he saw the men whisper among themselves.

"Thanks," spoke the driver of the car, and he threw in the gears. As the big machine darted ahead, the goggles which one of the men wore slipped off. Tom had a glimpse of his face.

"Amberson Morse!" he exclaimed as they drove away. "If that isn't the man who was sneaking around dad's motor shop he's his twin brother! I wonder if those men aren't after the patent model. I must be on my guard!"

Tom, watching the car fade out of sight on the road ahead of him, slowly started his motorcycle.

He was much puzzled and alarmed.

TOM SWIFT and His Motorcycle

———

CHAPTER XIII

CAUGHT IN A STORM

THE MORE TOM tried to reason out the men's actions, the more he kept coming back to his encounter with the tramp. And the harder he endeavored to seek a solution to that odd puzzle, the more complicated it all seemed. He rode on until he saw the town of Thessaly spreading out below him. With the view came a new idea.

"I'll go get a good lunch," he decided, "and perhaps that will help me to think more clearly. That's what dad always does when he's puzzling over an invention." He was soon seated in a restaurant, backpack beside him in another chair, where he ate a substantial meal.

His insistence on keeping the pack with its secret contents gave the waiter some consternation, so Tom finally had to take the manager aside and explain some of his situation without going into details,. As the Swift name was well known and well respected in Thessaly, no more was said about the matter.

"I'm just going to stop puzzling over this matter," he decided. "I need to push an to Albany and tell the lawyer, Mr. Crawford, what has happened. Perhaps he can advise me."

Once this decision was made Tom felt better.

"That's just what I needed," he thought, "someone to shift the responsibility upon. I'll let the lawyers do the worrying. That's what they're paid for. Now for Albany, and I hope I don't have to stop, except for supper, until I get there. I'll need to do some night riding to make up for lost time, but I've got a powerful lamp, and the roads from here on are good."

Tom was soon on his way again. The highway leading to Albany was a hard, tarmacadam one, and he fairly flew along the level stretches passing almost all of the occasional cars on the road.

"This is making good time," he thought. "I won't be so very late after all, assuming that nothing delays me."

The young inventor looked up into the sky. The sun, which had been shining brightly all day, was now hidden behind a mass of hazy clouds, for which the rider was duly grateful, as it was becoming quite warm.

"It's more like summer than I thought," said Tom to himself. "I won't be surprised if we get rain tomorrow."

Another look at the sky confirmed this belief, and he had not gone on many more miles when his opinion suddenly changed. There was a dull rumble in the west, and Tom noticed that a bank of low-lying clouds had formed; the black, inky masses of vapor being whirled upward as if by some powerful blast.

"Guess my storm is going to arrive ahead of time," he said. "I've heard that this new surface can get slippery when it is very wet. I'd better look for shelter."

With a suddenness that characterizes summer showers, the

whole sky darkened. The thunder increased, and the flashes of lightning became more frequent and dazzling. A wind sprang up and blew clouds of dust from the roadside up into Tom's face.

"It certainly is going to be a good thunder storm," he admitted. "I'm bound to be delayed now. Well, there's no help for it. If I get to Albany before midnight I'll be doing well."

A few drops of rain splashed on his hands, and as he looked up to note the state of the sky others fell in his face. They were big drops, and where they splashed next to the road they formed little globules of mud.

"Best head for that big tree," thought Tom "It will give me some shelter. I'll wait there—" His words were interrupted by a deafening crash of thunder which followed close after a blinding flash.

"No tree for me!" murmured Tom. "I forgot that they're dangerous in a storm. Tall things always get hit by lightning before low ones. I wonder where I can stay?"

He turned on all the power possible and sprinted ahead. Around a curve in the road he went, leaning over to preserve his balance, and just as the rain came pelting down in a torrent he saw ahead of him a white church on the suddenly deserted road. To one side was a long shed, where the farmers typically left their their teams when they came to service.

"Just the thing!" cried the boy, "and just in time!"

He turned his motorcycle into the yard surrounding the church, and a moment later had come to a stop beneath the shed. It was broad and long, furnishing good protection against the storm which had now burst in all its fury.

Tom was not very wet, and checked to see that the model, which was partly of wood, had suffered no damage. Finding that it's protective wrapping had protected it, he gave his attention to his machine.

"Seems to be all right," he murmured. "I'll just oil her up while I'm waiting. This can't last long, it's raining too hard."

He busied himself over the motorcycle, adjusting a nut that had been rattled loose, and putting some oil on the bearings and the chain.

Next, he used his small oil can spout to dribble some lubrication into the rubber tubing that encased his control cables. Giving each of the levers a few squeezes, Tom was satisfied that they would remain free and easy when he could get back onto the road.

He wiped away some grime where a little oil had mixed with dust and road grit, then dried the saddle, and soon had the motorcycle practically gleaming.

The rain kept up steadily. Once he had completed his attentions to his machine, he moved over to the rear wall and sat on the dry ground. All of his pushing and struggling with the motorcycle had served to tire his back and arms, so he stretched a bit to loosen them.

Rising a minute later, Tom strode forward and looked out from under the protection of the shed.

"It certainly is coming down for keeps," he murmured. "This trip is a regular hoodoo so far. Hope I have it better coming back."

As he looked down the road he spotted an automobile coming through the mist of rain. It was an open car, and he saw the three men in it huddled up under the insufficient protection of some blankets.

Tom said aloud, "They'd ought to come in here. There's plenty of room. Maybe they don't see it. I'll call to them."

The car was almost opposite the shed and it slowed to a stop. Tom was about to call out when one of the men in the auto looked over. He saw the shelter and spoke to the chauffeur. The latter was preparing to steer up into the shed when the two men on the rear seat caught sight of Tom standing at the front.

Words were exchanged and the car stopped once more. Although he could make out no individual words, Tom could tell by the tones that floated through the downpour that a small argument was breaking out among the auto's occupants.

He opted to withdraw his head and to move back a few feet into the shelter.

The argument went on for almost two minutes until all of the men suddenly ceased speaking.

Tom believed it must be a trick of the darkness and the rain, but he thought he saw one of the men pull a shiny object out of a coat pocket and point it in his direction.

The other occupant of the rear seat grabbed the man's arm and he put the object back inside his coat.

"That's the same car that passed me a while ago," said the young inventor half aloud. "The one with the three men who seem to be after dad's patent. It looks as if one has a gun. I hope they don't—"

He did not finish his sentence, for at that instant the chauffeur quickly swung the machine around and headed it back into the road. Clearly the men were not going to take advantage of the shelter of the shed.

"That's mighty strange," murmured Tom. "They certainly saw me. As soon as they did, they turned away. Can they be afraid of me?"

He went to the edge of the shelter and peered out. The auto had disappeared down the road, now hidden behind a veil of rain. Shaking his head over the strange occurrence, Tom went back to where he had left his motorcycle.

"Things are getting more and more muddled," he said. "I'm positive those were the same men, and yet—"

He shrugged his shoulders. The puzzle was getting beyond him. And, it appeared that danger was lurking straight ahead.

TOM SWIFT and His Motorcycle

———

CHAPTER XIV

ATTACKED FROM BEHIND

STEADILY the rain came down, the wind driving it under the shed until Tom was hard put to find a place where the drops did not reach him. He withdrew into a far corner, taking his motorcycle and backpack with him.

There, sitting on a chunk of wood under the rough mangers where the horses were fed while the farmers attended church, the lad thought over his situation. He could make little of it, and the more he tried the worse it seemed to become. He looked out across the wet landscape.

"I wonder if this is ever going to stop?" he mused. "It looks as if we are in for an all-day downpour, yet we ought only to have a summer shower by rights."

Tom got up and went to the far side of the shelter, looking for anything with which he might cover himself. Giving up, he returned to his log.

"I guess what *I* think about it won't influence the weather a bit. I might as well make myself comfortable. Can't do anything. Let's see." Tom put his mind to computing his future travels." If I get to Fordham by six o'clock I ought to be able to make Albany by nine, as it's only forty miles. I'll get supper in Fordham, and push on. That is, I will if the rain stops."

He knew that he could avoid using any more time than it took to eat one of his own sandwiches, but he would prefer the warmth and comfort of a restaurant.

But, waiting out the weather was the most necessary matter to deal with first. Tom rose from his seat and strolled over to the front of the shed to look out.

"I believe it is getting lighter in the west," he told himself. "Yes, the clouds are lifting. It's going to clear. It's only a summer shower, after all."

But just as he said that there came a sudden squall of wind and rain, fiercer than any which had preceded. Tom was driven back to his seat on the log. It was quite a cold wind driving the rain. Tom, still slightly damp, shivered. As he sat back on his log, he noticed that there was a big opening in the rear of the shed near his seat. A couple of boards were off showing the small graveyard behind the church and shed.

"This must be a drafty place in winter," he observed. "If I could find a drier spot I'd sit there, but this seems to be the best," and he remained there, musing on many things. In the midst of his thoughts he imagined he heard the sound of an automobile approaching. "I wonder if its those men coming back?" he exclaimed. "If they are—"

The youth again arose, and went to the front of the shed. He could see nothing, and moved back to escape the rain. There was little doubt that the shower would soon be over. Looking at his watch, Tom began to calculate when he might arrive in Albany.

He was busy trying to figure out the best plan to pursue,

and was hardly conscious of his surroundings. Twice he felt his head roll forward as weariness brought him near to crowsing.

Seated on the log, with his back to the opening in the shed, the young inventor did not see or hear the figure stealthily creeping toward him, through the wet grass. Nor had he seen the automobile that had come to a stop in back of the horse shelter—an automobile containing two rain-soaked men, who were anxiously watching the one stealing through the grass.

Something registered in His mind, and Tom opened his eyes and put his watch back into his pocket. He looked out into the storm. It was almost over. The sun was trying to shine through the clouds, and only a few drops were falling. The youth stretched with a yawn. He was tired of sitting still.

At the moment when he raised his arms to relieve his muscles something was thrust through the opening behind him. It was a long club, and an instant later it descended on the lad's head. He went down in a heap, limp and motionless.

Through the opening leaped a man. He bent over Tom, looked anxiously at him, and then, stepping to the place where the boards were off the shed, he motioned to the men in the automobile.

They got out and hurried from the machine.

"I knocked him out, all right," observed the man who had reached through and dealt Tom the blow with the club.

"Knocked him out! I should say you did, Simpson!" exclaimed one who appeared better dressed than the others. "Have you killed him?"

"No, and I wish you wouldn't mention my name, Mr. Anderson. I—I don't like—"

"Nonsense, Simpson. No one can hear us. But I'm afraid you've hit him far too hard. I didn't want him harmed, you fool."

"Oh, I guess Simps—Featherton knows how to do it, Anderson," commented the third man. "He's had experience that way, eh, Featherton?"

"Yes, Mr. Morse, but if you please I wish you wouldn't mention my past."

"All right, Featherton, I know what you mean," rejoined the man addressed as Morse. "Now let's see if we have drawn a blank or not. I believe he has with him the very thing we want."

"Doesn't seem to be about his person," observed Anderson, as he carefully felt about the clothing of the unfortunate Tom.

"Very likely not. It's too bulky. But there's his motorcycle over there. It looks as if what we want may be in that pack sitting on top of the saddle. Jove, Featherton, but I think he's coming to!"

Tom stirred uneasily and moved his arms, while a moan came from between his parted lips.

"I've got some stuff that will fix him!" exclaimed the man addressed as Featherton, and who had been operating the automobile. He took something from his pocket and leaned over Tom. In a moment the young inventor was still again.

"Quick now, see if it's there," directed Morse, and Anderson hurried over to the machine.

"Here it is!" he called. "I'll take it to our car, and we can get away."

"Are you going to leave him here like this?" asked Morse.

"Yes, why not?"

"Because someone might have seen him come in here, and also remember that we, too, came in this direction."

"What would you do?"

"Take him down the road a way and leave him. We can find some shed near a farmhouse where he and his machine will be out of sight until we get far enough away. Besides, I don't like to leave him so far from help, unconscious as he is."

"Oh, you're getting chicken-hearted," said Anderson with a sneer. "However, have your way about it. I wonder what has become of Jake Burke? He was to meet us in Thessaly, but he did not show up."

"Oh, I wouldn't be surprised if he had trouble dressed in that tramp rig he insisted on adopting. I told him he was running a risk, but he said he had masqueraded as a tramp before."

"So he has. He's pretty good at it. Now, Simpson, if you will —"

"Not Simpson! You both agreed to call me Featherton," interrupted the chauffeur, turning to Morse and Anderson.

"Ah, so we did. I forgot that this lad met us one day, and heard me call you Simpson," admitted Morse. "Well, Featherton it shall be. But we haven't much time. It's stopped raining, and the roads will soon be well traveled. We must get away. So, if we are to take the lad and his machine to some secluded place, we'd better be at it. No use waiting for Burke. He can look out after himself. Anyhow, we have the model now, and there's no use in him hanging around Swift's shop, as he intended to do, waiting for a chance to sneak in after it. Anderson, if you and Simpso—sorry, I mean Featherton—will carry young Swift here, I'll shove his motorcycle along to the auto, and we can put it and him in."

The two men, first looking through the hole in the shed to make sure they were not observed, went out, carrying Tom, who was no light load. Morse followed them, pushing the motorcycle, and carrying under one arm the knapsack containing the valuable model.

"I think this is the time we get ahead of Mr. Swift," murmured Morse, pulling the tip of his black mustache, when he and his companions had reached the car in the field. "We have just what we want now."

"Yes, but we had hard enough work getting it," observed Anderson. "It was pure luck that we saw this lad come in here, or we would have had to chase all over for him, and maybe then we would have missed him. Hurry, Simpson—I mean Featherton. It's getting late, and we've got lots to do."

The chauffeur sprang to his seat with Anderson taking his place beside him. The motorcycle was tied on behind the big touring car. With the unconscious form of Tom in the tonneau beside Morse, who stroked his mustache nervously, the auto started off.

The storm had passed, and the sun was shining brightly, but Tom could not see it.

TOM SWIFT and His Motorcycle

———

CHAPTER XV

A SEARCH IN VAIN

SEVERAL HOURS later, Tom had a curious dream. He imagined he was wandering about in the polar regions, and that it was very cold. He was trying to reason with himself that he could not possibly be on an expedition searching for the North Pole, still he felt such an incredibly icy wind blowing over his body that he shivered. He shivered so hard, in fact, that he shivered himself awake.

He could feel a cold, hard surface beneath him. He opened first one eye and then the other. As he tried to pierce the darkness that enveloped him, he was momentarily startled to find he had a fleeting idea that perhaps he *had* wandered off to some unknown country.

It was quite dark and cold, wherever he might be. He was in a daze, yet noticed that there was a strange and vaguely familiar smell around him—an odor that he tried to recall. He sniffed the air and then his clothes. Finally, he cupped his lower face and smelled. It was on his face!

At once, it came to him what it was—chloroform.

Barton Swift had undergone an operation a year earlier, and chloroform was used to deaden his pain. His recovery room had reeked of it.

"I've been chloroformed!" exclaimed the young inventor, and his words sounded strange in his ears. "That's it. I've met with an accident riding my motorcycle. I must have hit my head, for it hurts fearfully and I have gone blind. Oh, why didn't I finish that helmet? Someone picked me up, carried me to a hospital and they have operated on me. I wonder if they took off an arm or leg? I wonder what hospital I'm in? Why is it so dark and cold?"

As he asked himself these questions his brain gradually cleared from the haze caused by the cowardly blow, and from the chloroform that had been administered by Featherton.

Tom's first tentative act was to feel first of one arm, then the other. Having satisfied himself that neither of these were missing or mutilated he reached down to his legs.

"They're all right, too," he murmured. "I wonder what they did to me? That's certainly chloroform I smell, and my head feels as if someone has sat on it. Or in it. I wonder—"

Quickly he put up his hands to his head. He felt all around it. There appeared to be nothing the matter with it, except that there was quite a lump on the back, where the club had struck.

"I seem to be all here," went on Tom now patting down his torso. He was much mystified. "But where am I? That's the question. It's a funny hospital, so cold and dark—"

Just then his hands came in contact with the cold ground on which he was lying.

"I'm outdoors!" he exclaimed feeling the dirt and grass on which he lay.

Then in a flash it all came back to him—how he had gone to wait under the church shed until the rain was over.

"I fell asleep, and now it's night," the youth went on. "No wonder I am sore and stiff. And that chloroform—" He could not account for that, and he paused, puzzled once more. Then he struggled to a sitting position. His head was strangely dizzy, but he persisted, and got to his feet.

He could see nothing, and groped around In the dark, until he thought to strike a match. Fortunately he had a number in his pocket. As the little flame flared up Tom started in surprise.

"This isn't the church shed!" he exclaimed. "And, I'm not blind. It's much smaller here than the shed! I'm in a different place! Great Scott! but what has happened to me?"

The match burned Tom's fingers and he dropped it. The darkness closed in once more, but Tom was used to it by this time, and looking ahead of him he could make out that the shed was an open one, similar to the one where he had taken shelter. He could see the sky studded with stars, and could feel the cold night wind blowing in.

"My motorcycle!" he exclaimed in alarm. "The model of dad's invention—the papers!"

Our hero thrust his hand into his pocket. The papers were gone! Hurriedly he lit another match. It took but an instant to glance rapidly about the small shed. His machine was not in sight!

Tom felt his heart sink. After all his precautions he had been robbed. The precious model was gone, and it had been his proposition to take it to Albany in this manner. What would his father say?

The lad lit match after match, and made a rapid tour of the shed. The motorcycle was not to be seen. But what puzzled Tom more than anything else was how he had been brought from the church shed to the one where he had awakened from his stupor.

"Let me try to think," said the boy, speaking aloud, for it seemed to help him. "The last I remember is seeing that automobile, with those mysterious men in, approaching. Then it disappeared in the rain. I thought I heard it again, but I couldn't see it. I was sitting on the log, and—and—well, that's all I can remember. I wonder if those men—"

The young inventor paused. Like a flash it came to him that the men were responsible for his predicament. They had somehow knocked him insensible, stolen his motorcycle, the papers and the model, and then brought him to this place, wherever it was. Tom was a shrewd reasoner, and he soon evolved a theory which later learned was the correct one.

He reasoned out almost every step in the crime of which he was the victim, and at last came to the conclusion that the men had stolen up behind the shed and attacked him.

"Now, the next question to settle," spoke Tom, "is to learn where I am. How far did those scoundrels carry me, and what has become of my motorcycle?"

He walked toward the point of the shed where he could observe the stars gleaming, and there he lighted some more matches, hoping he might see his machine.

By the gleam of the little flame he noted that he was in a farmyard, and he was just puzzling his brain over the question as to what city or town he might be near when he heard a voice shouting, "Here, what you lightin' them matches for? You want to set the place afire? Who be you, anyhow—a tramp?"

It was unmistakably the voice of a farmer, and Tom could hear footsteps approaching on the run.

"Who be you, I said?" the voice repeated. "I'll have the constable after you in a jiffy if you're a tramp. You git off my property!"

"I'm not a tramp," called Tom promptly. "I've met with an accident. Where am I?"

"Humph! Mighty funny if you don't know where you are," commented the farmer. "Jed, fetch me a lantern so as I can take a look at who this is."

"All right, pop," answered another, slightly dull-sounding voice. A moment later Tom saw a tall man standing in front of him.

"I'll give you a look at me without waiting for the lantern," said Tom quickly, and he struck a match, holding it so that the gleam fell upon his face.

"Salted mackerel! It's a young feller!" exclaimed the farmer. "Who be you, anyhow, and what you doin' here?"

"That's just what I would like to know," said Tom, passing his hand over his head, which was still paining him. "Am I near Albany? That's where I started for this morning."

"Albany? You're a good way from Albany," replied the farmer. "You're in the village of Dunkirk."

"How far is that from Thessaly?"

"About seventy miles."

"As far as that?" cried Tom. "They must have carried me a good way in their automobile."

"Was you in that automobile?" demanded the farmer.

"Which one?" asked Tom quickly.

"The one that stopped down the road just before supper. I seen it, but I didn't pay no attention to it. If I'd 'a' knowed you fell out, though, I'd 'a' come to help you sooner."

"I didn't fall out of it, Mr.—er—" Tom paused.

"Blackford is my name, Amos Blackford."

"Well, Mr. Blackford, My name is Tom Swift. And, I didn't fall out. I was drugged by three men and brought here against my will."

"Drugged! Salted mackerel! But there's been a crime committed, then. Jed! Boy, you hurry up with that lantern an' git your deputy sheriff's badge on. There's been druggin' an' all sorts of crimes committed. I've caught one of the victims. Hurry up!" he yelled into the darkness. "My son's a deputy sheriff," he added, by way of an explanation to Tom.

"Then I hope he can help me catch the scoundrels who robbed me," said Tom.

"Robbed you, did they? Hurry up, Jed. There's been a robbery! We'll rouse the neighborhood an' search for the villains. Hurry up, Jed!"

"I'd rather find my motorcycle, and a valuable model which was with it, than locate those men," went on Tom. "They also took some papers from me."

"Didn't see none of that, but I was a fair distance from that automobile of theirs. What was you doin' before they captured you?"

Tom told how he had started for Albany earlier that day, adding his theory of how he had been attacked and carried away in the auto. The latter part of it was borne out by the testimony of Mr. Blackford.

"What I know about it," said the farmer, when his son Jed had arrived on the scene with a lantern and his badge, "is that jest about supper time I saw an automobile stop down the road a bit. Maybe a couple hunnert feet or so. It was gittin' dusk, an' I saw some men git out. I didn't pay no attention to them, 'cause I was busy about the milkin'. The next I knowed I seen some one strikin' matches in my wagon shed, an' I come out to see what it was."

"Did you see who they were?" Tom asked.

Shaking his head, Mr. Blackford admitted that they had left before he had arrived at the shed. "Saw one of them heading back down the road, though. Had on one of them round hats. Bowler or somethin' like that."

Tom nodded. The man he had first seen in the post office had worn a bowler. It was all fitting together in his mind.

"Those men must have brought me all the way from the church shed near Thessaly to here," declared Tom. "Then they lifted me out and put me in your shed. Maybe they left my motorcycle also."

"I didn't see nothin' like that," said the farmer. "Is that what you call one of them two-wheeled lickity-split things that a man sits on the middle of an' goes like chain-lightning?"

"It is," said Tom. "I wish you'd help me look for it."

The farmer and his son agreed, and other lanterns having been secured, a search was made.

After about half an hour the motorcycle was discovered in some bushes at the side of the road, near where the automobile had stopped. Though some of the gasoline appeared to have leaked out, it seemed to be in fine condition.

But, the backpack and model was missing from it, and a careful search near where the machine had been hidden did not reveal them.

Nor did as careful a hunt as they could make in the darkness disclose any clues to the scoundrels who had drugged and robbed Tom.

TOM SWIFT and His Motorcycle

———

CHAPTER XVI

BACK HOME

"WE'VE GOT TO organize a regular searchin' party," declared Jed Blackford, after he and his father, together with Tom and the farmer's hired man, had searched up and down the road by the light of lanterns.

"We'll organize a posse an' have a regular hunt. This is the worst crime that's been committed in this district in many years, an' I'm goin' to run the scoundrels to earth."

"Don't be talkin' nonsense, Jed," interrupted his father. "You won't catch them fellers in a hunnert years. They're miles an' miles away from here by this time in their automobile. All you can do is to notify the sheriff. I guess we'd better give this young man some attention. Let's see, you said your name was Quick, didn't you?"

"No, but it's very similar," answered Tom with a smile. "It's Swift."

"I knowed it was something had to do with speed," went on Mr. Blackford. "Wa'al, now, suppose you come in the house an' have a hot cup of tea. You look sort of draggled out."

Tom was glad enough to avail himself of the kind invitation, and he was soon in the comfortable kitchen, relating his story, with more detail, to the farmer and his family. Mrs. Blackford applied some home-made remedies to the lump on the youth's head, and it felt much better.

"I'd like to check over my motorcycle," he said, after his second cup of tea. "I need to see if those men damaged it any. If they have, I'm going to have trouble getting back home to tell my father of my bad luck. Poor dad! He will be very much worried when I tell him the model and his patent papers have been stolen."

"It's too bad!" exclaimed Mrs. Blackford. "I wish I had hold of them scoundrels!" and her previously-gentle face bore a severe frown. "Of course you can have your thing-a-ma-bob in to see if it's hurt, but please don't start it in here. They make a terrible racket."

"No, I'll look it over in the woodshed. All I'll need is a lantern or two," promised Tom. "If it's all right I think I'll start back home at once."

"No, you can't do that," declared Mr. Blackford. "You're in no condition to travel. You might fall off an' git hurt. It's nearly ten o'clock now. You jest stay here all night, an' in the mornin', if you feel all right, you can start off. I couldn't let you go tonight."

Indeed, Tom did not feel very much like undertaking the journey, for the blow on his head had made him dizzy, and the chloroform still made him feel slightly ill. Mr. Blackford wheeled the motorcycle into the wood house, which opened from the kitchen, and there the youth went over the machine.

He was glad to find that it had sustained no damage. In the meanwhile Jed had gone off to tell the startling news to near-by farmers. Quite a throng, with lanterns, went up and down the road, but all the evidence they could find were the marks of the automobile wheels, which clues were not very helpful.

"But we'll catch them in the mornin'," declared the deputy sheriff. "I'll know that automobile again if I see it. It was painted red."

"That's the color of a number of automobiles," said Tom with a smile. "I'm afraid you'll have trouble identifying it by that means. I am surprised, though, that they did not carry my motorcycle away with them. It is a valuable machine."

"They were afraid to," declared Jed. "It would look odd to see a machine like that in an auto. Of course when they were going along country roads in the evening it didn't much matter, but when they headed for the city, as they probably did, they knew it would attract suspicion to 'em. I know, for I've been a deputy sheriff 'most a year."

"I believe you're right," agreed Tom. Inside, he knew that his captors would be many, many miles away by now and any promise made of catching them the next day was merely posturing. "They didn't dare take the motorcycle with them, but they hid it, hoping I would not find it. I'd rather have the model and the papers, though, than half a dozen motorcycles."

"Maybe the police will help you find them," said Mrs. Blackford. "Jed, you must telephone the police the first thing in the morning. It's a shame the way criminals are allowed to go on. If honest people did those things, they'd be arrested in a minute, but it seems that scoundrels can do as they please."

"You wait, I'll catch 'em!" declared Jed confidently. "I'll organize another posse in the mornin'."

"Well, I know one thing, and that is that the place for this young man is in bed!" exclaimed motherly Mrs. Blackford, and she insisted on Tom retiring. He was somewhat restless at first—mainly from the effects of the tea—and the thought of the loss of the model and the papers preyed on his mind.

Finally, utterly exhausted, he sank into a heavy slumber, and did not awaken until the sun was shining in his window the next morning. A good breakfast made him feel somewhat better, and he was more like the resourceful Tom Swift of old when he went to get his motorcycle in shape for the ride back to Shopton.

"Well, I hope you find those criminals," said Mr. Blackford, as he watched Tom oiling the machine. "If you're ever out this way again, stop off and see us."

"Yes, do," urged Mrs. Blackford, who was getting ready to churn. Her husband looked at the old-fashioned barrel and dasher arrangement, which she was filling with cream.

"What's the matter with the new churn?" he asked in some surprise.

"It's broken," she replied. "It's always the way with those new-fangled things. It works ever so much nicer than this old one, though," she went on to Tom, "but it gets out of order easy."

"Let me look at it," suggested the young inventor. "I know something about machinery. And, I must find some way to repay your kindness."

The churn, which worked by a system of cogs and a handle, was brought from the woodshed. It was an inexpensive model from a company that competed with his father's design.

Tom soon saw what the trouble was. One of the cogs, held in place by a thin wooden peg,had become displaced. It did not take him five minutes with the tools he carried on his motorcycle, to put it back into place, devise a stronger pin from a piece of wood the farmer supplied, and the churn was ready to use.

"Well, I declare!" exclaimed Mrs. Blackford. "You are handy at such things!"

"Oh, it's just a knack," replied Tom modestly. "Now that

I've put a stronger plug in there, and the cog wheel won't come loose again. The manufacturer ought to have done that. I imagine lots of people have this same trouble with these churns."

"Indeed they do," asserted Mrs. Blackford. "Sallie Armstrong has one, and it got out of order the first week they had it. I'll let her look at mine, and maybe her husband can fix it."

"I'd go and do it myself, but I want to get home," said Tom, and then he showed her how, by inserting a stronger plug in a certain place, there would be no danger of the cog coming loose again.

"It may not be my place, but if anyone is in need of buying a new churn I would suggest the Swift Churn. It only costs about two dollars more and is built to last for years." Tom hoped that he might raise a little business for his father. It would never repay the loss over the model and patent papers, though.

"That's certainly slick!" exclaimed Mr. Blackford. "Well, I wish you good luck, Mr. Swift, and if I see those scoundrels around this neighborhood again I'll make 'em wish they'd let you alone."

"That's right," added Jed, polishing his badge with his big, red handkerchief.

Mrs. Blackford transferred the cream to the repaired churn which Tom had fixed. As he rode off down the highway on his motorcycle, she waved one hand to him, while with the other she operated the handle of the apparatus.

"Now for a quick run to Shopton to tell dad the bad news," spoke Tom to himself as he turned on full speed and dashed away. "My trip has been a failure so far."

TOM SWIFT and His Motorcycle

CHAPTER XVII

MR. SWIFT IN DESPAIR

TOM WAS THINKING of many things as his speedy machine carried him mile after mile nearer home. By noon he was over half way on his journey, and he stopped in a small village for his lunch.

"I think I'll make inquiries of the police here, to see if those men might have traveled this direction," decided Tom as he left the restaurant. "Though I am inclined to believe they kept on to Albany, or even into New York City, where they have their headquarters. They will want to make use of dad's model as soon as possible, though what they will do with it I don't know." He tried to telephone to his father, but could get no connection, as the wire was being repaired.

"Wish I knew who to wire in Washington about dad's invention. I'll bet the Navy could pt a stop to anyone trying to register that patent!"

The police force of the place where Tom had stopped for lunch was like the town itself—small and not of much consequence. The chief constable, not what you could call a chief of police, had heard of the matter from the general alarm sent out in all directions from Dunkirk, where Mr. Blackford lived.

"You don't mean to tell me you're the young man who was chloroformed and robbed!" exclaimed the constable, looking at Tom as if he doubted his word.

"I'm the young man," declared Tom. "Have you seen anything of the thieves?"

"Not a thing, though I've instructed both my men to keep a sharp lookout for a red automobile with three scoundrels in it. My men are to make an arrest on sight."

"*How many* men have you?"

"Two," he repeated his rather surprising answer. "We generally have three but one has to work on a farm daytimes, so I ain't really got but the two in what you might call active service on a full time basis."

Tom restrained a desire to laugh. At any rate, the aged constable meant well.

"One of my men seen a red automobile, a little while before you come in my office," went on the official, "but it wasn't the one wanted, 'cause a young woman was running it all alone. It struck me as rather curious that a woman would trust herself all alone in one of them things, wouldn't it you?"

"Oh, no, women and young ladies often operate them," said Tom. "They are all the rage in larger cities."

"I should think you'd find one handier than the two-wheeled apparatus you have out there," went on the constable, indicating the motorcycle, which Tom had stood up against a tree.

"I may have one some day," replied the young inventor. "But I guess I'll be moving on now. Here's my address, in case you hear anything of those men. But I don't imagine you will."

"Me either. Fellows as slick as them are won't come back this way and run the chance of being arrested by my men. I have two on duty nights," he went on proudly, "besides myself, so you see we're pretty well protected."

Tom thanked him for the trouble he had taken, and was soon on his way again. He swept on along the quiet country roads anxious for the time when he could consult with his father over what would be the best course to take.

When Tom was about a mile away from his house he saw in the road ahead of him a rickety old wagon. A second glance at it told him the outfit belonged to Eradicate Sampson, for the animal drawing the vehicle was none other than the mule, Boomerang.

"But what in the world is Rad up to?" mused Tom. The black man was out of the wagon and was going up and down in the grass at the side of the highway in a curious fashion. "I guess he's lost something," decided Tom.

When he got nearer he saw what Eradicate was doing. The colored man was pushing a lawn-mower slowly to and fro in the tall, rank grass that grew beside the thoroughfare. At the sound of Tom's motorcycle he looked up. There was such a woe-begone expression on his face that Tom at once stopped his machine and got off.

"What's the matter, Rad?" Tom asked.

"S'mattah, Mistah Swift? Why, dere's a pow'ful lot de mattah, an' dat's de truff. I'se been swindled, dat's what I has."

"Swindled? How?"

"Well, it's dis-a-way. Yo' see dis here lawn-moah? Dis mis'able 'scuse for a lawn-moah?"

"Yes, it doesn't seem to work," and Tom glanced critically at it. As Eradicate pushed it slowly to and fro, the blades did not revolve, and the wheels slipped along on the grass.

"No, sah, it doan't work, an' dat's how I've been swindled, Mistah Swift. Yo' see, I done traded mah ole grindstone off for dis here lawn-moah, an' I got stuck."

"What, that old grindstone that was broken in two, and that you fastened together with concrete?" asked Tom, for he had seen the outfit with which Eradicate, in spare times between cleaning and whitewashing, had gone about the country, sharpening knives and scissors. "You don't mean that old, broken one?"

"Dat's what I mean, Mistah Swift. Why, it was all right. I mended it so dat de break wouldn't show, an' it would sharpen things if yo' run it slow. But dis here lawn-moah won't wuk slow ner fast."

"I guess it was an even exchange, then," went on Tom. "You didn't get bitten any worse than the other fellow did."

"Yo' doan s'ppose yo' kin fix dis here moah so's I kin use it, Mistah Swift?" asked Eradicate, not bothering to go into the ethics of the matter. "I reckon now with summah comin' on I kin make mo' with a lawn-moah than I kin with a grindstone —dat is, ef I kin git it to wuk. I jest got it a while ago an' decided to try it, but it won't cut no grass."

"I haven't much time," said Tom, "and I'm anxious to get home, but I'll take a quick look at it."

Tom leaned his motorcycle against the fence. He could no more pass a bit of broken machinery, which he thought he could mend, than some men and boys can pass by a baseball game without stopping to watch it, no matter how pressed they are for time.

It was Tom's hobby, and he delighted in nothing so much as tinkering with machines, from lawn mowers to steam engines.

Tom took hold of the handle, which Eradicate gladly relinquished to him, and his trained touch told him at once what was the trouble.

"Some one has had the wheels off and put them on wrong, Rad," he said. "The ratchet and pawl are reversed. This mower would work backwards, if that were possible."

"Am dat so, Mistah Swift?"

"That's it. All I have to do is to take off the wheels and reverse the pawl."

"I—I didn't know mah lawn-moah was named Paul," said the handy man. "Is it writ on it anywhere?"

"No, it's not the kind of Paul you mean," said Tom with a laugh. "It's spelled differently. A pawl is a sort of catch that fits into a ratchet wheel and pushes it around. In your mower it is the piece of metal that catches to the wheels and then lets the blade turn only in the correct direction. I'll have it fixed in a jiffy for you."

Tom worked rapidly. With a monkey-wrench he removed the two big wheels of the lawn-mower and reversed the pawl in the cogs. In five minutes he had replaced the wheels, and the machine, except for needed sharpening, did good work.

"There you are, Rad!" exclaimed Tom at length.

"Yo' shuh am a wonder at inventin'!" cried the man gratefully. "I'll cut yo' grass all summah fo' yo' to pay fo' this, Mistah Swift."

"Oh, that's too much. I didn't do a great deal, Rad."

"Well, yo' saved me from bein' swindled, Mistah Swift, an' I shuh does 'preciate dat."

"How about the fellow you traded the cracked grindstone to, Rad?"

"Oh, well, ef he done run it slow it won't fly apart, an' he'll do dat, anyhow, fo' he shuh am a lazy man. I guess we is about even there, Mistah Swift."

"All right," spoke Tom with a laugh. "Sharpen it up, Rad, and start in to cut grass. It will soon be summer," and Tom, leaping upon his motorcycle, was off like a shot.

He found his father in his library, reading a book on scientific matters. Mr. Swift looked up in surprise at seeing his son.

"What! Back so soon?" he asked. "You did make a flying trip. Did you give the model and papers to Mr. Crawford?" Seeing the sad look on his son's face, he asked, "Are you all right?"

"No, Dad, I was robbed yesterday. Those scoundrels got ahead of us, after all. They knocked me out and stole your model. I tried to telephone to you, but the wires were down, or something."

"What!" cried Mr. Swift. "Oh, Tom! That's bad! I will lose thousands of dollars if I can't get that model and those papers back!" and with a despairing gesture Mr. Swift rose and began to pace the floor.

He stopped suddenly and turned to face Tom.

"Oh, dear!" he exclaimed. "What will the Navy do if our enemies gain control of that turbine!"

TOM SWIFT and His Motorcycle

———

CHAPTER XVIII

HAPPY HARRY RETURNS

TOM WATCHED his father anxiously. The young inventor knew the loss had been a heavy one, and he blamed himself for not having been more careful. He felt sick to his stomach with worry.

"Tell me all about it, Tom," said Mr. Swift at length, after taking a deep breath. "Are you sure the model and papers are gone? How precisely did it happen?"

Tom related what had befallen him leaving out no detail.

"Oh, my!" cried Mr. Swift. "Are you certain you are not hurt, Tom? Shall I send for the doctor?" For the time being his anxiety over his son was greater than that concerning his loss.

"No, Dad. I'm all right now. I got a bad blow on the head, but Mrs. Blackford fixed me up. I'm awfully sorry—"

"No! Now don't say another word," interrupted Mr. Swift, holding up a hand. "It wasn't your fault. It might have happened to me. Or anyone those men might have associated with the model. I dare say it would, for those scoundrels seemed very determined. They are desperate, and will stop at nothing to make good the loss they sustained on the patent motor they exploited. Now they will probably try to make use of my model and papers."

"Do you think they'll do that, Dad?"

"Yes. They will either make a motor exactly like mine, or construct one so nearly similar that it will answer their purpose. I will have no redress against them, as my patent is not fully granted yet. Mr. Crawford was to attend to that."

"Can't you do anything to stop them, Dad? File an injunction, or something like that? Call the Navy or the War Department?"

"I don't know. I must see Mr. Crawford at once. I wonder if he could come here? He might be able to advise me. I have had little experience with legal difficulties. My specialty is in other lines of work. But I must do something. Every moment is valuable. I wonder where those men are? You're certain they were the same three?"

"I'm sure one of them was the same man who came here that night—the man with the black mustache—who dropped the telegram," said Tom. "I had a pretty good look at him as the auto passed me, and I'm sure it was he. Of course I didn't see who it was that struck me down, but I imagine it was some one of the same gang."

"Very likely. Well, Tom, I must do something. I suppose I might telegraph to Mr. Crawford—he will be expecting you in Albany—" Mr. Swift paused musingly. "No, I have it!" he suddenly exclaimed. "I'll go to Albany myself."

"Go to Albany, Dad?"

"Yes, I must explain everything to the lawyers and then he can advise me what to do. Fortunately I have duplicate papers of those you took, which I can show him. They bear the date of completion of the turbine along with a small mark of verification that I devised. Of course regaining the originals will be necessary before I can prove my claim."

Can't Mr. Crawford take the drawings to the Patent Office and at least get those registered?"

His father shook his head, sadly. "The loss of the model is the most severe. Without that, I can do little. I will have Mr. Crawford take whatever steps are possible, but it is the model upon which the patent is checked and then approved. No model—no patent!" He straightened up, saying "I'll take the night train, Tom. I'll have to leave you to look after matters here, and I needn't caution you to be on your guard. Though, having got what they were after, I imagine those financiers, or their minions, will not bother us again."

"Very likely not," agreed Tom, "but I will keep my eyes open just the same. Oh, but that reminds me, Dad. Did you see anything of a tramp around here while I was away?"

"A tramp? No, but you had better ask Mrs. Baggert. She usually attends to them. She's so kind-hearted that she frequently gives them a good meal."

The housekeeper, when asked into the front room and queried, said that no tramps had applied for assistance in the last few days.

"Why do you ask, Tom?" inquired his father.

"Because I had an experience with one, and I believe he was a member of the same gang who robbed me." Tom told of his encounter with Happy Harry, and how the latter had purposely broken the wire on the motorcycle. "He did it to waylay me, I'm sure. Or, at least to delay me until the rest of the gang would locate me."

"You had a narrow escape," commented Mr. Swift. "If I had known the dangers involved I would never have allowed you to take the model to Albany. We would have traveled together at the very least."

"Well, I didn't take it there, after all," said Tom with a grim smile.

"I must hurry and pack my valise," went on Mr. Swift. "Mrs. Baggert," he called out, "we will have an early supper, and I will start at once for Albany."

"I wish I could go with you, Dad, to make up for the trouble I caused," spoke Tom.

"Now Tom. Don't talk that way," advised his father kindly. "I will be glad of the trip. It will ease my mind to be doing something."

Tom felt rather lonesome after his father had left, but he laid out a plan of action for himself that he thought would keep him occupied until his father returned. In the first place he made a tour of the house and various machine shops to see that doors and windows were securely fastened.

"What's the matter? Do you expect burglars, Master Tom?" asked Garret Jackson, the aged engineer when Tom checked on his boiler room.

"Well, Garret, you never can tell," replied the young inventor, and he told a greatly-shortened version of his experience and the necessity for Mr. Swift going to Albany. "Some of those scoundrels, after finding how easy it was to rob me, may try it again and get some at dad's other valuable models. I'm taking no chances."

"That's right, Master Tom. I'll keep steam up in the boiler tonight, though we don't really need it, as your father told me you would probably not run any machinery when he was gone. But with a good head of steam up, and a hose handy, I can give any burglars a hot reception. I almost wish they'd come, so I could get square with them."

"I don't, Garret. They are not pleasant men and there is no telling what they might stoop to. I guess everything is in good shape. If you hear anything unusual, or the alarm goes off during the night, call me."

"I will, Tom," and the old engineer, who had a living space in a shack adjoining the boiler room, locked the door after Tom left.

The young inventor spent the early evening in attaching a new wire to his motorcycle to replace the one he had purchased while on his disastrous trip. The temporary one was not just the proper thing, though it answered well enough.

Then, he turned to the matter of the hemet. Though he had practically ruined the leather one when his drilling had caused the hard coating to crack and shatter, he believed that he might be able to use it as a form on which he could create a slightly larger helmet.

He began by coating the helmet using candle wax. Whatever he applied he could be sure to have it release once the wax was heated over a flame.

Tom thought for many minutes before coming to the decision to try making a new inner form out of papier maché. He hurredly tore a great number of strips of that day's paper and mixed up some flour and water glue. In just a few minutes he had created a new helmet shape. He placed it next to a heater in his shed and waited for it to become partly dry.

Before it hardened completely, Tom eased it away and off of the old helmet. The wax worked perfectly for nothing stuck or become misshapen. He set the paper form neat the heater while he located and mixed another batch of the polymer.

He drilled several holes in the top, sides and back of the form before applying the first coat of polymer. It flowed around the drilled edges and sealed the hole edges.

Over the next several hours Tom applied more coats to the inside and outside of the helmet. After five coats he decided to call it an evening. He measured the thickness and found that he had built up the helmet to better than a quarter inch.

It also felt much lighter than the previous one. "Leather is obviously heavier than paper," he mused to himself as he locked up and headed to the house.

Mrs. BAggert fixed Tom a small dinner of potatoes and eggs. As she was cooking the meal he made a full round of the house checking all doors and windows.

He ate the meal with relish as he found he had become very hungry, having had nothing to eat in over eight hours.

Soon, Tom felt that it was time to go to bed, as he was tired. He made a second round of the house, looking to doors and windows, until Mrs. Baggert exclaimed, "Oh, Tom, do stop! You make me nervous, going around that way. I'm sure I shan't sleep a wink tonight, thinking of burglars and tramps."

Tom laughingly desisted, and went up to his room. He sat up a few minutes, writing a letter to a girl of his acquaintance in Shopton. In spite of the fact that the young inventor was very busy with his own and his father's work, he found time for lighter pleasures. Then, as his eyes seemed determined to close of their own accord if he did not let them, he tumbled into bed.

Tom fancied it was nearly morning when he suddenly awoke with a start. He heard a noise, and at first he could not locate it. Then his trained ear traced it to the dining-room.

"Mrs. Baggert must be getting breakfast, and is rattling the dishes," he thought. "But why is she up so early?"

It was quite dark in Tom's room, save for a little gleam from the crescent moon outside, and by the light of this Tom arose and looked at his watch.

"Two o'clock," he whispered. "That can't be Mrs. Baggert, unless she's sick, and got up to take some medicine."

He listened intently. Below, in the dining-room, he could hear stealthy movements.

"Mrs. Baggert would never move around like that," he

decided. "She's too heavy and makes the floorboards creak. If it's a burglar—or one of that gang has gotten in—I'm going to catch him at it!"

Hurriedly he slipped on some clothes and then took up a small rifle he kept in one corner. He made sure it was loaded. Then, with a small electric flashlight of the kind used by police men, and sometimes by burglars, he started on tiptoe toward the lower floor.

As Tom softly descended the stairs he could more plainly hear the movements of the intruder. He made out now that the burglar was in Mr. Swift's study, which opened from the dining-room.

"He's after dad's papers!" thought Tom. "I wonder which one this is?"

The youth had often gone hunting in the woods, and he knew how to approach cautiously. Thus he was able to reach the door of the dining-room without being detected. He had no need to flash his light, for the intruder was swinging his around so frequently that Tom could see him perfectly. The fellow was working at the safe in which Mr. Swift kept his more valuable papers.

Softly, very softly Tom brought his rifle to bear on the back of the thief. Then, holding the weapon with one hand, for it was very light, Tom extended the electric flash, so that the glare would be thrown on the intruder and would leave his own person in the black shadows. Pressing the spring which caused the battery lantern to throw out a powerful glow, Tom focused the rays on the kneeling man.

"That will be about all!" the youth exclaimed in as steady a voice as he could manage.

The burglar turned like a flash, eyes wide in terror. Tom had a good look at the man's face. It was the tramp—Happy Harry!

TOM SWIFT and His Motorcycle

———

CHAPTER XIX

TOM ON THE HUNT

TOM HELD his rifle steady, though he only intended it as a means of intimidation and would not have fired at the burglar except to save his own life. But the sight of the weapon was enough for the tramp. He crouched motionless. His own light had gone out when it dropped from his hand. By the gleam of the torch he carried, Tom could see that the man held some tool with which he had been endeavoring to force the safe.

"I guess you've got me!" exclaimed the intruder, and there was no trace of the tramp dialect.

"It looks like it," agreed Tom grimly. "Drop that bar! Are you a tramp now, or in some other disguise?"

"Can't you see?" asked the fellow sullenly, and then Tom did notice that the man still had on his tramp clothes, minus his beard.

"What do you want?" asked Tom.

"Hard to tell," replied the burglar calmly. "I hadn't got the safe open before you came down and disturbed me. I'm after money, naturally."

"No, you're not!" exclaimed Tom.

"What?" and the man seemed surprised.

"No, you're not!" went on Tom, and he held his rifle in readiness. "You're after the patent papers and the model of the turbine motor. But it's gone. Your confederates got it away from me. They probably haven't told you yet, and you're still on the hunt for it. You'll not get it, but I've got you."

"Ah. I see," admitted Happy Harry, and he spoke with some culture. "If you don't mind," he went on, "would you just move that gun a little? It's pointing right at my head, and it might go off."

"It is going off—very soon!" exclaimed Tom grimly, and the tramp's eyes opened in alarm. "Oh, I'm not going to shoot *you*," continued the young inventor. "so long as you stand there. I'm going to fire this as an alarm, and our engineer will come in here and tie you up. Then I'm going to hand you over to the police. This rifle is a repeater, and I am a pretty good shot. I'm going to fire once now, to summon assistance. If you try to get away I'll be ready to fire again in a second, and that one will be meant for you. I've caught you, and I'm going to hold on to you until I get that model and those papers back."

"Oh, you are, eh?" asked the burglar calmly. "Well, all I've got to say is that you have grit. Go ahead. I'm caught good and proper. I was foolish to come in here, but I thought I'd take a chance."

"Who are you, anyhow? Who are the men working with you to defraud my father of his rights?" asked Tom somewhat bitterly.

"I'll never tell you," answered the burglar. "I was hired to do certain work, and that's all there is to it. I'm not going to tattle on my associates."

"We'll see about that!" burst out Tom. Then he noticed that

a dining-room window behind where the burglar was kneeling was open. Doubtless the intruder had entered that way, and intended to escape in the same manner.

"I'm going to shoot," announced Tom, and, aiming his rifle at the open window where the bullet would do no damage, he pressed the trigger.

He noticed that the burglar was crouching low down on the floor, but Tom thought nothing of this at the time. He imagined that Happy Harry—or whatever his name was— might be afraid of getting hit.

There was a flash of fire and a deafening report as Tom fired. The cloud of smoke obscured his vision for a moment. As the echoes died away Tom could hear Mrs. Baggert screaming in her room.

"It's all right!" cried the young inventor reassuringly. "No one is hurt, Mrs. Baggert!" Then he flashed his light on the spot where the burglar had crouched. As the smoke rolled away Tom peered in vain for a sight of the intruder.

Happy Harry was gone!

Holding his rifle in readiness in case he should be attacked from some unexpected quarter, Tom strode forward. He flashed his light in every direction. There was no doubt about it. The intruder had fled. Taking advantage of the noise when the gun was fired, and under cover of the smoke, the burglar had leaped from the open window.

Tom guessed as much. He hurried to the casement and peered out, at the same time noticing the cut wire of the burglar alarm. It was quite dark, and he fancied he could hear the noise of someone running rapidly. Aiming his rifle into the air, he fired again, at the same time crying out, "Hold on!"

"All right, Tom, I'm coming!" called the voice of the engineer from his shack. "Are you hurt? Is Mrs. Baggert murdered? I hear her screaming."

"That's pretty good evidence that she isn't murdered," said Tom with a grim smile.

"Are you hurt?" again called Mr. Jackson.

"No, I'm all right," answered Tom. "Did you see anyone running away as you came up?"

"No, I didn't. What happened?"

"A burglar got in, and I had him cornered, but he got away when I fired to rouse you."

By this time the engineer was at the stoop, onto which the window opened. Tom unlocked a side door and admitted Mr. Jackson, and then, the overhead light having been turned on, the two looked around the room. Nothing in it had been disturbed, and the safe had not been opened.

"I heard him just in time," commented Tom, telling the engineer what had happened. "I wish I had thought to get between him and the window. Then he couldn't have gotten away."

"He might have injured you, though," said Mr. Jackson. "Know if he had a gun or a knife? We'll go outside now, and look—"

"Is any one killed? Are you both murdered?" cried Mrs. Baggert standing at the dining room door. "If any one is killed I'm not coming in there. I can't bear the sight of blood."

"No one is hurt," declared Tom with a laugh. "Come on in, Mrs. Baggert," and the housekeeper entered, peeking through her fingers, her hair all done up in curl papers.

"Oh, my goodness me!" she exclaimed. "When I heard that cannon go off I was sure the house was coming down. How is it someone wasn't killed?"

"That wasn't a cannon, it was only my little rifle," said Tom, and then he told again, for the benefit of the housekeeper, the story of what had happened.

"We'd better hurry and look around the premises," suggested Mr. Jackson. "Maybe he's hiding and planning to come back. He has some confederates on the watch."

"Not much danger of that," declared Tom. "Happy Harry is far enough away from here now, and so are his confederates, if he had any, which I doubt. Still, it will do no harm to take a look around."

A search resulted in nothing, and the Swift household had soon settled down again, though no one slept soundly during the remainder of the night.

In the morning Tom sent word of what had happened to the police of Shopton. Some officers came out to the house, but beyond looking at the window by which the burglar had entered and at some footprints in the garden, they could do nothing. Tom wanted to go off on his motorcycle on a tour of the surrounding neighborhood to see if he could get any clues, but he did not think it would be wise in the absence of his father. He thought it would be better to remain at home, in case any further efforts were made to get possession of valuable models or papers.

"There's not much likelihood of that, though," said Tom to the old engineer. "Those fellows have what they want, and are not going to bother us again."

The engineer inquired what it was they had, but Tom kindly refused to tell him on the grounds that his father wanted it kept a secret that even Mrs. Baggert did not know. This satisfied the man and he returned to tend to his boiler.

"I sure would like to get that model back for dad, though." Tom thought. "If they file it and take out a patent, even if he can prove that it is his, it will mean a long lawsuit and he may be defrauded of his rights, after all. Possession is nine points of the law, and part of the tenth, too, I guess."

So Tom remained at home and busied himself as well as he could.

He began with an examination of his new helmet. Though it had slightly slumped in on the top, Tom tried it on and believed that it fit even better that way. He tested the strength with his leather-wrapped hammer and was able to give it several moderate blows without it showing any sign of damage.

He threaded two pieces of leather through holes he had made for the purpose of creating a chin strap to hold the helmet onto his head. A simple buckle made the think complete, so he gave it a coat of bright red paint.

"That will ensure that they see me coming," he said to himself as he admired the work.

Next, Tom set about repairing and improving the alarm system that had failed to pass muster the night before. It operated on the principle that a cut wire would fail to pass its current along. This registered in a simple vacuum tube circuit and sounded the alarm bells. The wires were also set to disconnect from their points in the trees and shrubbery surrounding the property should someone walk into one or more of them. This also set off the bells to alert the household.

He examined the wire that had been cut; the wire that had been placed in front of the window used by Happy Harry. It had been neatly cut, but not before Harry had twisted a new length of wire onto it at two points and cut between them. Even when Harry had cut the wire, it allowed the current to continue passing through and so did not set off the alarm.

Tom knew that he could devise, with his father's assistance, something that could measure minute changes in the current such as when a wire was being touched or had been lengthened. But, that would need to come later. He replaced the cut wire with a new piece.

One thing he could do was to pass a greater amount of electricity through the wires. He reasoned that anyone touching the wires would now get a painful shock that might deter them from continuing their plans.

He did the necessary wiring work and also created the proper step-down transformer so that the vacuum tubes in the detector circuit would not burn out.

He received a telegram from his father that afternoon, stating that Mr. Swift had safely arrived in Albany, and would return the following day.

"Did you have any luck, Dad?" asked the young inventor, when his father, tired and worn from the unaccustomed traveling, reached home in the evening.

"Not much, Tom," was the reply. "Mr. Crawford has gone back to Washington, and he is going to do what he can to prevent those men taking advantage of me, but I fear that it may be too little too late."

"Did you get any trace of the thieves? Does Mr. Crawford think he can?"

"No to both questions. His idea is that the men will remain in hiding for a while, and then, when the matter has quieted down, they will proceed to get a patent on the turbine motor that I invented. That is, of course, if patenting it is their primary concern. There is still the possibility that this is a theft by a foreign power. In that case we should well pray that it is never used against us in war."

"But, in the meanwhile, can't you make another model and get a patent yourself?"

"No, there are certain legal difficulties in the way that I do not fully comprehend. Besides, those men have the original papers I need. As for the model, it might take me nearly a year to build a new one that will turn and interact properly. It is very complicated. I am afraid, Tom, that all my labor on the turbine motor is lost. Those scoundrels will reap the benefit of it and our nation may suffer because of it."

"Oh, Dad! Then it is all my fault. If I had only taken a different road instead of the old wood road. If I had not stopped when the rain came. Those criminals would have never found me. You must think that you can never trust me again," Tom wailed.

Barton Swift took his son into a hug and said, "I'm sure those fellows will be caught. Between the police all around the state and folks watching out in Washington..." he left the rest unsaid.

Tom pulled away, saying, "Now that you are back home again, I'm going out on a hunt on my own account. I don't put much faith in the police. It was through me, Dad, that you lost your model and the papers, and I'll get them back!"

"No, you must not think it was your fault, Tom," said his father. "You could not help it, though I appreciate your desire to recover the missing model."

"And I'll do it, too, Dad. I'll start tomorrow, and I'll make a complete circuit of the country for a hundred miles around. I can easily do it on my motorcycle. If I can't get on the trail of the three men who robbed me, maybe I can find Happy Harry. I'll bet he knows where they are."

"I doubt it, my son. Still, you may try. I advise you to be ultra cautious, though. Now, I must write a note to Mr. Crawford and tell him about the attempted burglary while I was away. It may give him a clue to work on. I'm afraid you ran quite a risk, Tom."

"I didn't think about that, Dad. I only wish I had managed to keep that rascal a prisoner."

The next day Tom started off on a hunt. He planned to be gone overnight, as he intended to go first to Dunkirk, where Mr. Blackford lived, and begin his search from there.

TOM SWIFT and His Motorcycle

CHAPTER XX

ERADICATE SAWS WOOD

THE FARMER'S family, including the son who was a deputy sheriff, was glad to see Tom. Jed said he had "been on the job" ever since the mysterious robbery had taken place. Though he had seen many red automobiles pass through the area he had seen no trace of the three men.

After making a more detailed, daylight search of the vicinity in which his motorcycle had been abandoned Tom decided that there was little to be gained from remaining in the area.

From Dunkirk Tom traveled the most likely route the men would have taken from the point of the old church shed to Dunkirk. As he rode along he looked for any possible clues. As he suspected, there were none. Anything that might have been useful, such as tire tracks, had been washed away by the rains that evening.

He made some inquiries in the neighborhood of the church shed where he had taken shelter. The locality was sparsely settled, however, and no one could give any clues to the robbers. There had been nobody in the church that day and no one had visited the little graveyard. It was another dead end.

The young inventor next made a trip over the lonely, sandy road where he had met with the tramp, Happy Harry. But there were even fewer houses near that stretch than around the church, so he got no satisfaction there. Tom spent the night at a small country inn, and resumed his search the next morning but with no results. The men had apparently completely disappeared, leaving no traces behind them.

"I may as well go home," thought Tom, as he was riding his motorcycle along a pleasant country road. "Dad may be worried. Something may have turned up in Shopton that will aid me. If there isn't, I'm going to start out again in a few days in another direction."

There was no news in Shopton, however. Town found his father scarcely able to work he was so worried over the loss of his most important invention.

Tom felt miserable but could think of nothing to do.

Two weeks passed, the young machinist taking trips of several days' duration to different points near his home, in the hope of discovering something. But he was unsuccessful.

In the meantime, no reassuring word was received from the lawyers in Washington. Mr. Crawford wrote that no move had yet been made by the thieves to take out patent papers, and while this was some consolation to Mr. Swift, he could not proceed on his own account to protect his new turbine. All that could be done was to await the first movement on the part of the scoundrels.

"I think I'll try a new plan tomorrow, Dad," announced Tom one night when he and his father had talked over again, for perhaps the twentieth time, the happenings of the last few weeks.

"What would that be, Tom?" asked the inventor.

"Well, I think I'll take a week's trip on my machine. I'll visit all the small towns around here. Instead of asking in houses for news of the tramp or his confederates, I'll go directly to the police and constables. I'll ask if they have arrested any tramps recently. If they have, I'll ask them to let me see their 'hobo' prisoners."

"What good will that do?"

"I have an idea that though the burglar who got in here may not be a regular tramp. He certainly disguises himself like one at times, and may be known to other tramps. If I can get on the trail of Happy Harry I may locate the other men. Tramps are a suspicious lot and would be very likely to remember such a peculiar chap as Happy Harry. It may take a few coins, but I am sure that they will tell me where they had last seen him. Then I will have a starting point."

"Well, that may be a good plan," assented Mr. Swift. "At any rate it will do no harm to try. A tramp locked up in a country police station will very likely be willing to talk. Go ahead with that scheme, Tom, but don't get into any danger. How long will you be away?"

"I don't know. A week, perhaps, maybe longer. I'll take plenty of money with me, and stop at country hotels overnight."

"What protection can you take along? I am worried that you may fall to another bout of foul play."

Tom thought a moment. "For starters, I will have my new helmet." He had shown it to Mr. Swift the week before and the older man had been well impressed with its sturdiness. "I also plan to take along a gadget I have been working on for some little time. It utilizes a storage battery, a pocket-sized class B battery of 90-volts along with a transformer I have made out of very thin wire. That increases the voltage to almost 600-volts. It feeds into a hand-held applicator that uses two electrodes to pass the current into whatever it touches."

Mr. Swift had been following Tom's description keenly. "If I understand the principle, then should you touch the applicator to a person the full 600-volt shock would pass into them. That wouldn't kill them, would it?"

Tom grinned. "No. They will get a shock that might knock their socks right off, but it would only be temporary. As soon as you pull the electrodes away, they would be all right. A bit dazed, though."

He admitted to his father that he had tried it on himself the previous day. Noting his father's alarm, Tom told him, "It only really made the muscles in my arms and legs go all wobbly. They stayed that way only a few seconds. I'll wager that it would keep an attacker stunned for long enough to escape."

Tom lost no time in putting his plan into execution. He packed some clothes in a small case, which he attached to the rear of his motorcycle. Having said good-bye to his father, he started off.

The first three days he met with no success. He located several tramps in country lock-ups, where they had been sent for begging or loitering, but none of them knew Happy Harry or had ever heard of a tramp answering his description.

"He ain't one of us, youse can make book on dat," said one "hobo" whom Tom interviewed. "No real knight of de highway goes around in a disguise. We leaves dat for de story-book detectives. I'm de real article, I am, an' I don't know no Happy Harry. But, fer dat matter, any of us is happy enough in de summer time, so long as we don't strike a burgh like dis, where dey jugs you fer simple panhandlin'."

In general, Tom found the tramps willing enough to answer

his questions, though some were sullen, and returned only surly growls to his inquiries. Whenever one gave him any response, he rewarded that man with a fifty-cent piece. in all it had cost him five dollars to find out very little of any use.

"I guess I'll have to give it up and go back home," he decided one night. But there was a small town about nine miles from Shopton which he had not yet visited, and he resolved to try there before returning.

Accordingly, the next morning found him inquiring of the police authorities in Meadtown. But no tramps had been arrested in the last month, and no one had seen anything of a tramp like Happy Harry or three mysterious men in an automobile.

Tom was beginning to despair. Riding along a silent road, that passed through a strip of woods, he was trying to think of some new line of action, when the silence of the highway that had resounded only with the muffled sound of his machine, was broken by several exclamations.

"Now, Boomerang, yo' might jest as well start now as later," Tom heard a voice saying—a voice he recognized well. He pulled over. "Yo' has got t' do dis here wurk, an' dere ain't no gittin' out of it. Dis here wood is got to be sawed, an' yo' has got to saw it. But it is jest laik yo' to go back on yo' ole friend Eradicate in dis here fashion. I neber could tell what yo' were gwine t' do next, an' I cain't now. G'l dang, now, git along won't yo'? Let's git dis here sawmill started."

Tom shut off the power and leaped from his motorcycle. From the woods at his left came the protesting "hee-haw" of a mule.

"Boomerang and Eradicate Sampson!" exclaimed the young inventor. "What can they be doing here?"

He leaned his motorcycle against the fence and advanced toward where he had heard the voice of the colored man. In a little clearing he saw them. Eradicate was presiding over a portable sawmill, worked by a treadmill, on the incline of which was the mule, its ears laid back, and an unmistakable expression of anger on its face."Why, Rad, what are you doing?" cried Tom.

"Good land o' mersy! Ef it ain't young Mistah Swift!" cried the black man. "Howdy, Mistah Swift! Howdy! I'm jest tryin' t' saw some wood, t' make a livin', but Boomerang he doan seem t' want t' help," and with that Eradicate looked reproachfully at the animal. Boomerang returned his stare.

"What seems to be the trouble, and how did you come to own this sawmill?" asked Tom.

"I'll tell yo', Mistah Swift, I'll tell yo'," spoke Eradicate. "Sit right here on dis log, an' I'll explanate it to yo'."

"The last time I saw you, you were preparing to go into the grass-cutting business," went on Tom.

"Yes, sah! Dat's right. So I was. Yo' has got a memory, yo' shuh has. But it is dis here way. Grass ain't growin' quick enough, an' so I traded off dat lawn-moah an' bought dis here mill. But now it won't go, an' I shuh am in trouble," and once more Eradicate Sampson looked indignantly at Boomerang.

"Tell me all about it," urged Tom sympathetically, for he had a friendly feeling toward the aged black man.

"Well," began Eradicate, "I shuh thought I were gwine to make money cuttin' grass, 'specially after yo' done fixed mah moah. But 'peared laik nobody wanted any grass cut. I trabeled all over, an' I couldn't git no jobs. Now me an' Boomerang has to eat, no mattah ef he is contrary, so I had t' look fo' some new wuk. I traded dat lawn-moah off fo' a cross-cut saw, but dat was such hard wuk dat I gib it up. Den I got a chance to buy dis here outfit cheap, an' I bought it."

Eradicate then went on to tell how he had purchased the portable sawmill from a man who had no further use for it, and how he had managed to transport it from a distant village to the spot where Tom had met him. There, he had secured permission to work a piece of woodland on shares, sawing up the smaller trees into cord wood. He had started in well enough, cutting down considerable timber, for he was a willing worker. It was when he tried to start his mill he met with trouble.

"I counted on Boomerang helpin' me," he said to Tom. "All he has to do is walk on dat tread mill, an' keep goin'. Dat makes de saw go 'round, an' I saws de wood. But de trouble is dat I can't git Boomerang to move. I done tried ebery means I knows on him, an' he won't go. I talked kind to him, an' I talked harsh. I done whackeded him wif a stick, an' I rub his ears soft laik, an' he allers laik dat fine, but he won't go. I fed him on carrots an' I gib him sugar, an' I eben starve him, but he won't go. Here I been tryin' fo' three days now t' git him started, an' not a stick has I sawed. De man I'm wukin' wif on shares he git mad, an' he say ef I doan saw wood pretty soon he gwine t' git annuder mill here. Now I ax yo' fair, Mistah Swift, ain't I got lots of trouble?"

"You certainly seem to have," agreed Tom "But why is Boomerang so obstinate? Usually on a treadmill a horse or a mule has to work whether they like it or not. If they don't keep moving the platform slides out from under them, and they come up against the back bar."

"Dat's what done happened to Boomerang," declared Eradicate. "He done back up against de bar, an' dere he stay.He plants hims bottom on de bar and hims feets out in front, an' he doan move."

Tom went over and looked at the mill. The outfit was an old one, and had seen much service, but the trained eye of the young inventor saw that it could still be used effectively. Boomerang watched Tom, as though aware that something unusual was about to happen.

"Here I done gone an' 'vested mah money in dis here mill," complained Eradicate, "an' I ain't sawed up a single stick. Ef I wasn't so kind-hearted I'd chastise dat mule wuss dan I has, dat's what I would."

Tom said nothing. He was stooping down, looking at the gearing that connected the tread mill with the shaft which revolved the saw. Suddenly he uttered an exclamation,

"Rad, have you been monkeying with this machinery?" he asked.

"Me? Good land, Mistah Swift, no, sah! I wouldn't tetch it. It's jest as I got it from de man I bought it oh. It worked when he had it, but he used a hoss. It's all due to de contrariness of Boomerang, an' if I—"

"No, it isn't the mule's fault at all!" exclaimed Tom. "The mill is out of gear, and tread is locked, that's all. The man you bought it off probably did it so you could haul it along the road. I'll have it fixed for you in a few minutes. Wait until I get some tools."

From the bag on his motorcycle Tom got his implements. He first unlocked the treadmill, so that the inclined platform on which the animal slowly walked could revolve. No sooner had he done this than Boomerang, feeling the slats under his hoofs moving away, started forward. With a rattle the treadmill slid around.

"Good land o' massy! It's goin'!" cried Eradicate delightedly. "It shuh is a-going'!" he added as he saw the mule, with nimble feet, send the revolving, endless string of slats around and around. "But de saw doan move, Mistah Swift. Yo' is pretty smart at fixin' it as much as yo' has, but I reckon it's too busted t' eber saw any wood. I'se got bad luck, dat's what I has."

"Nonsense!" exclaimed Tom. "The sawmill will be going in a moment. All I have to do is to move it into gear. See here,

Rad. When you want the saw to go you just throw this handle forward. That makes the gears mesh."

"What's dat 'bout mush?" asked Eradicate.

"Mesh—not mush. I mean it makes the cogs fit together. See," and Tom interlaced his fingers to demonstrate the concept, then he pressed the lever. In an instant, the saw began revolving.

"Hurrah! Dere it goes! Golly! see de saw move!" cried the delighted colored man. He seized a stick of wood, and in a trice it was sawed through.

"Whoop!" yelled Eradicate. "I'm sabed now! Bless yo', young Mistah Swift, yo' suttinly is a wondah!"

"Now, I'll show you how it works," went on Tom. "When you want to stop Boomerang, you just pull this handle. That locks the tread, and he can't move it," and, matching the action to his words, Tom stopped the mill. "Then," he went on, "when you want him to move, you pull the handle this way," and he showed the black man how to do it. In a moment the mule was moving again. Then Tom illustrated how to throw the saw in and out of gear, and in a few minutes the sawmill was in full operation, with a most energetic colored man feeding in logs to be cut up into stove lengths.

"You ought to have an assistant, Rad," said Tom, after he had watched the work for a while. "You could get more done then, and move on to some other wood patch."

"Dat's right, Mistah Swift, so I had oughter. But I 'done tried, an' couldn't git any. I ast seberal men, but dey'd radder whitewash an' clean chicken coops. I guess I'll has t' go it alone. I ast a white man yisterday ef he wouldn't like t' pitch in an' help, but he said he didn't like to wuk. He was a tramp, an' he had de nerve to ask me fer money—me, a hard-wukin' black man."

"You didn't give it to him, I hope."

"No, indeedy, but he come so close to me dat I was askeered he might take it from me, so I kept hold of a club. He shuh was a bad-lookin' tramp, an' he kept laffin' all de while, like he was happy."

"What's that?" cried Tom, struck by Rad's words. "Did he have a thick, brown beard?"

"Dat's what he had," answered Eradicate, pausing in the midst of his work. "He shuh were a funny sort of tramp. His hands done looked laik he neber wuked, an' he had a funny blue ring one finger, only it weren't a reg'lar ring, yo' know. It was pushed right inter his skin, laik a man I seen at de circus once, all cobered wid funny figgers."

Tom leaped to his feet.

It had to be Happy Harry!

TOM SWIFT and His Motorcycle

———

CHAPTER XXI

ERADICATE GIVES A CLUE

"WHICH FINGER was the blue ring tattooed on?" Tom asked, and he waited anxiously for the answer.

"Let me see, it were on de right—no, it were on de little finger of de left hand."

"Are you sure, Rad?"

"Shuh, Mistah Swift. I took p'tic'lar notice, 'cause he carried a stick in dat same hand."

"It must be my man—Happy Harry!" exclaimed Tom half aloud. "Which way did he go, Rad, after he left you?"

"He went up de lake shore," replied the colored man. "He asked me if I knowed of an ole big house up dere, what nobody libed in, an' I said I did. Den he left, an' I were glad of it."

"Which house did you mean, Rad?"

"Why, dat ole mansion what General Harkness used t'

lib in befo' de wah. Dere ain't nobody libed in it fo' some years now, an' it's deserted. Fallin' down I s'pose. Maybe a lot of tramps stays in it, an' dat's where dis man were goin'."

"Maybe," assented Tom, who was all excitement now. "Just where is this old house, Rad?"

"Away up at de head of Lake Carlopa. I useter wuk dere befo' de wah, but it's been a good many years since quality folks libed dere. Dat was back when my daddy an my mammy was slaves. Well, they weren't no slaves, ach'lly. They's freeborn colored, but they's wukkin' lak they's slaves. Why, did yo' want t' see dat man, Mistah Swift?"

"Yes, Rad, I did, and very badly, too. I think he is the very person I want. But don't say anything about it. I'm going to take a trip up to that strange mansion. Maybe I'll get on the trail of Happy Harry and the men who robbed me. I'm much obliged to you, Rad, for this information. It's a good clue, I think. Strange that you should meet the very tramp I've been searching for."

"Well, I shuh am obliged to yo', Mistah Swift, fo' fixin' mah sawmill."

"That's all right. What you told me more than pays for what I did, Rad. i need you to promise me something. All right?"

"Shore, Mister Swift. Whatebers yo' wants."

"Unless it is my father or a policeman you know, please do not repeat anything about that man to anyone. Please?" Eradicate nodded his agreement. It is very important that that man not get any wind that we might be on to him or his whereabouts."

Sampson continued to nod while Tom spoke. In the end he crossed his finger over his heart and swore that nobody would get the information out of him.

Tom smiled and gently patted the man on the shoulder. "Thank you, Eradicate. You are a gentleman and I now am indebted to you. Well, I'm going home now to tell dad, and then I'm going to start out. Yesterday, you said it was, you saw Happy Harry?"

Rad nodded.

"Well, I'll get right after him," and leaving a somewhat surprised but very much delighted, man behind him, Tom mounted his motorcycle and started for home at a fast pace.

"Dad. I've got a clue!" exclaimed Tom, hurrying into the house not ten minutes later. "A good clue, and I'm going to start early in the morning to run it down."

"Wait a minute, now, Tom," cautioned his father slowly. "You know what happens when you get excited. Nothing good was ever done in a hurry."

"Well, I can't help being excited, Dad. I think I'm on the trail of those scoundrels. I almost wish I could start tonight."

"Suppose you tell me all about it," and Mr. Swift laid aside a scientific book he was reading.

Whereupon Tom began his tale. He told of each of the seeming dead ends he encountered on his long trip. How circumstances had provided no eye witnesses to practically anything he had done. He even related that the very waitress who had served him lunch that fateful day couldn't remember seeing him in the restaurant.

Finally, he told of his chance meeting with the black man, and what Eradicate had said about the tramp.

"But he may not be the same Happy Harry you are looking for," interposed Mr. Swift. "I am certain that there are tramps who don't like to work, which would explain the un-callused hands. And there are bound to be such men who have a jolly disposition. Also, there are those who ask for money and have designs tattooed on their hands. All very common."

"Oh, but I'm sure this is the same one," declared Tom. "He wants to stay in this neighborhood. At least until he locates his confederates. That's why he's hanging around. They haven't caught up with each other so he had to try to break into the house and your safe. He couldn't be sure. Now I have an idea that the deserted mansion where Eradicate used to work, and which once housed General Harkness and his family, is the rendezvous of this gang of thieves."

"You are still taking a great deal for granted, Tom."

"I don't think so, Dad. Real clues are turning out to be as rare as hen's teeth. If I expect to get anywhere on this, I've got to begin to assume something. Maybe I'm wrong, but I don't think so. At any rate, I'm going to try, if you'll let me."

"What do you mean to do?"

"I want to go to that deserted mansion and see what I can find. If I locate the thieves, well—"

"You may run into danger."

"Then you admit I may be on the right track, Dad?"

"Not at all," and Mr. Swift smiled inwardly at the quick

manner in which Tom turned the tables on him. "I admit there may be a band of tramps in that house. Very likely there is—almost any deserted place would be attractive to them. But they may not be the ones you seek. In fact, I hardly see how they can be. They might take quite the exception to you appearing in their midst. The men who stole my model and patent papers are wealthy. They would not be very likely to stay in deserted houses."

"Perhaps, but how many times do you hear about criminals throwing the police off their trail by doing unorthodox things? Isn't this just the sort of thing that nobody would think possible?"

"Well, there is something in that," admitted Mr. Swift, rubbing his jaw.

"And, we both know hove vital it is to recover your papers and the model from these men. I know that you haven't and can't tell me everything about it, but I just know that it is more important than just the money. We already have quite a bit of that." tom could see that his father was struggling with some inner conflict, so he decided to not press the matter.

You can say it and say it, but the fact is that it was me on the motorcycle and me with the important papers and the model who got shanghaied. I know that there are so many different possible outcomes, but in the end I lost all of that. Now, I have the opportunity to redeem myself. You know that I'll not take chances. We can even alert the police to stand by."

Mr. Swift thought it over for a moment and then nodded at Tom.

"Then I can go, Dad?"

"I suppose so. We must leave nothing untried to get back the stolen model and papers. You are correct to assume that there is something of a more vital nature to all this. I wish that I could tell you more, but there is some level of National security to this so I must remain silent, even to my own family. You may go, but I don't want you to run any risks. If you would only take some one with you. There's your chum, Ned Newton. Perhaps he would go."

Tom knew that Ned would never shirk from a fight. He was the most upstanding boy Tom knew. The two were made of the same moral values and were strong friend. As much as Tom would relish having Ned by his side, he realized that there was an inherent danger in his plan. He would rather face it alone that be responsible for Ned's wellbeing.

"No, I'd rather work this alone, Dad. I'll be careful. Besides, Ned could not get away from the bank. I may have to be gone several days. Perhaps up to a week. Besides, he has no motorcycle. If I need to escape quickly, then a second person behind me would only slow me down. I can manage all right."

Mr. Swift and his son sat in conversation for another hour going over Tom's plans and trying to find methods of overcoming possible obstacles.

Tom went up to bed well past ten that evening and had a restful and rewarding sleep knowing that he now had a way to redeem his previous mis-actions.

He set off bright and early taking both his electro-stunner gadget as well as a small signal rocket in case he needed to be rescued.

He had carefully laid his plans, and had decided that he would not go via a direct route to Pineford, the nearest village to the old Harkness mansion.

"If those fellows are in hiding up there, they may keep watch on who comes to the village," thought Tom. "The arrival of someone on a motorcycle will be sure to be reported to them, and they may skip out. I've got to come in from another direction, so I think I'll circle around and reach the mansion from the stretch of woods on the north."

He had inquired from Eradicate as to the lay of the land, and had a good general idea of it. He knew there was a patch of woodland on one side of the mansion, while the other sides were open.

To get to the woods,, he would need to ride a circuitous path beginning with a trek to the south and the town of The Glen. This would allow him to take an infrequently-traveled side road back to the east and then northward to Hague.

Once there, Tom planned to ride through Ticonderoga. From that point he could ride almost directly west and to the upper far side of Lake Carlopa. It was on that eastern side of the lake that the Harkness mansion lay.

"I may not be able to ride through the final mile or two of the woods," mused Tom, "but I'll take my machine as close as I can, and walk the rest of the way. Once I discover whether or not the gang is in the place, I'll know what to do."

TOM SWIFT and His Motorcycle

——

CHAPTER XXII

THE STRANGE MANSION

THOUGH TOM wanted to get to the possible location of his foes quickly, he knew that the plan he had laid down for himself meant that he must take the roundabout way. It would necessitate being a two whole days on the road, before he would be near the head of Lake Carlopa where the Harkness house was located. The lake was a large one, and Tom had never been to the upper end.

He had brought a small bedroll so that he might sleep in the woods that final night before attempting to approach his destination.

When he was within a few miles of Pineford on the first day, Tom took a road that branched off and went around it. "No use letting people from town to town see me. Now I wish that I dan painted my helmet a less-noticeable color."

Stopping at night in a lonely farmhouse where he was allowed the comfort of their barn, he pushed on the next morning, hoping to get to the woods that night. But a puncture to one of the tires delayed him, and after that was repaired he discovered something wrong with his batteries. He had to walk five miles out of his way to get new cells, and it was near nine when he finally pulled into the stretch of woods which he knew lay between him and the old mansion.

"I don't fancy starting in there at night," said Tom to himself. "Guess I'd better stay somewhere around here until morning, and then venture in. But the question is where to stay that will be out of sight of any hunters or passers-by?"

The country was deserted, and for a mile or more he had seen no houses. He drove on slowly for some distance farther, the lower speed making far less noise, and when he was about to turn back to retrace his way to the last farmhouse he had passed, he spotted a small shack at the side of the road.

"That's better than nothing, provided they'll take me in for the night," murmured Tom. "I'm going to ask, anyhow."

He found the shanty to be inhabited by an old man who made a living burning charcoal. Tom knew the theory behind the process. Wood was burned in an enclosed space with little or no air. All that was left when the burning was complete was the fairly-pure carbon remains that could be then re-burned to provide great amounts of heat.

The old man's equipment was build around an old water tank.

A brief look at the man's equipment told Tom that he was terribly inefficient. "He must lose better than half the wood that might become charcoal," he thought, and resolved to repay the man the next morning by showing him how to improve his output.

The shack was not very attractive, but Tom did not mind that. It would be better than a night in the open. Finding the charcoal-burner to be a kindly old fellow, they soon made a bargain with him to remain all night.

Tom slept soundly, in spite of his strange surroundings. After a simple breakfast in the morning he set about making a few adjustments to the man's equipment and helped to rig up a new valve and bypass pipes that would keep more air from infiltrating the enclosure and allow the man to burn off the resulting gas on which he might cook or heat water.

His host was in awe and promised to try it out that very day. Hw would endeavor to get word back to Tom of the success.

Tom inquired of the old man the best way of penetrating the forest.

After considering the matter for a moment and then consulting an old, stained map of the area, the man said, "You'd best strike right along the old lumberman's road. That leads right to the lake, and I think will take you to within a half mile or so of where you want to go. The old mansion is not set back too far from the lake shore."

As there were several large homes in the area, the man tried to describe to Tom the appearance of the Harkness place. "It has not as yet fallen into disrepair. Especially when viewed in partial darkness, you may not be able to quickly tell which house is the one you wish."

Before he departed, Tom learned that his destination was an imposing, three-floor home with a series of gables around the upper floor. It featured a porch that wrapped around the entirety of the house on the bottom floor and another around the second floor.

He thanked the man for his information and gave him two dollars for his hospitality. They parted with a friendly wave and Tom roared away on his motorcycle.

"Near the lake, eh?" mused Tom as he started off. He thought back to his run-in with one of the men, the one that had escaped by small boat. Tom smiled. If that didn't tie into his theory then nothing would. "That man probably came across the lake from near the Harkness place and I'll bet that's where he went back to," Tom thought to himself. "Now, I wonder if I'd better try to get to it from the water or the land side?"

He found it impossible to ride fast on the old lumberman's road. It was rutted and pitted with holes such that any speed greater than a fast walking pace meant that he could not steer clear of the many obstacles presented. When he judged he was so close to the lake that the noise of his motorcycle might be heard, he shut off the power, and walked along, pushing it. It was difficult traveling, but easier than the sandy road he had been on the last time he was forced to push his conveyance.

Within ten minutes he felt weary, but he kept on. Every half hour Tom stopped for a rest period of about ten minutes. This was just sufficient to let him press on for another period of walking.

At about noon was rewarded by a sight of something glittering through the trees, just a quarter of a mile ahead.

"That's the lake!" Tom exclaimed, half aloud. "I'm almost there."

A little later, having hidden his motorcycle in a clump of bushes, Tom grabbed his tool bag and made his way through the underbrush until he stood at the edge of the forest, just yards from the shore of Lake Carlopa. Cautiously, Tom looked about him. It was getting well on in the afternoon, and the sun was striking across the broad sheet of water.

Tom stepped forward a few paces and glanced up along the shore. Something amid a clump of trees caught his eyes. It was the chimney of a house. Skirting next to the trees, the young inventor walked a little distance along the lake shore. Coming around a slight corner he saw, looming up in the forest, a large building. It needed but a glance to show that it was the very house he was searching for. Though a fast glance from some distance would not give away its secrets, standing this close, Tom could see that it was practically falling into ruins.

There was no signs of life about it. Nor, for that matter, was there any life in the forest around him, or on the lake that stretched out before him.

"I wonder if that can be the place?" whispered Tom, for, somehow, the silence of the place was getting on his nerves. "It must be it," he went on. "It's just as Rad and the charcoal man described it."

He looked at the building with it's surrounding porches. The upper floor porch sagged in various places and Tom knew that it would not hold the weight of a man. There were placed on the lower porch that he feared would be so unstable that walking across them might prove to be hazardous as well.

He stood looking at it, the sun striking full on the mysterious mansion, hidden there amid the trees. He decided to walk back into the woods and to explore the surrounding area. Keeping close enough to view the house between the trees, Tom had soon arrived on the opposite side of the structure. During his walk he had noticed no signs of occupation; no lights or smoke from any of the five chimneys.

If the house had not completely matched what he expected, he might believe that it was then wrong house entirely. He lowered himself to the ground and crept forward to get closer for a better inspection.

By the time he had reached the very edge of the wooded area he began to detect signs of inhabitants. A pile of rotting rubbish sat behind the house, below an open window. "Surely, much of that is fairly new," he thought as it was giving off a terrible aroma. "Old trash doesn't smell like that!"

He worked his way back around to his initial starting point

taking mental note of the three other open or possibly missing windows on the bottom floor.

Suddenly, as making Tom look around to find its source, he heard the "putt-putt-putt" of a motorboat. He turned to one side, and saw, just pulling away from a little dock that he had not noticed before, a small craft.

It looked to be the same size and shape of the one that had been used in escaping him those weeks before. It contained one man—a dark-haired man, hunkered down in the middle. The man looked around him as he motored away and toward the middle of the lake.

No sooner had the young inventor caught a glimpse of him than is heart began to race in excitement. "That's the man who jumped over our fence and escaped with dad's papers!"

Then, before the occupant of the boat could catch sight of him, Tom turned and fled back into the bushes, out of view.

TOM SWIFT and His Motorcycle

———

CHAPTER XXIII

TOM IS PURSUED

TOM WAS so excited that he hardly knew what to do. His first thought was to keep out of sight of the man in the boat. The young inventor did not want the criminals to suspect that he was on their trail. To that end he hastily walked back until he knew he could not be seen from the lake. There he paused and peered through the bushes.

He caught another glimpse of the man in the motorboat. The craft was making fast time across the water. Tom was fascinated to see that the man was now all the way forward and appeared to be steering the little craft by leaning from side to side. His position also seemed to better balance the boat from front to back. It was making much better speed in this manner than Tom believed it would had the man been in the back.

"He didn't see me," murmured Tom with relief. "Lucky I saw him first. Now what should do?"

It was a hard question to answer. If he had some one with

169

whom to consult—such as his father—he would have felt better, but he knew he had to rely on himself. Tom was a resourceful lad, and he had often been obliged to depend on his wits.

But this time, very much was at stake and a false move might ruin everything.

"This is certainly the house," went on Tom, "and that man in the boat is one of the fellows who helped rob me. The next thing to do is to find out if the others of the gang are in the old mansion. If they are, I need to see if dad's model and papers are there. Then all I'll need to do is get myself plus our property away, and I fancy I'll have no easy job."

Tom had every reason to think this, for the men with whom he had to deal were desperate characters. They had already dared much to accomplish their ends and would do more before they would suffer defeat. Still, they would prove to under estimated the pluck of the lad who was pitted against them.

"I need to proceed on a specific plan, and have some system about this affair," he reasoned. "Dad is a great believer in developing a system, so I'll need to lay out a plan and see how nearly I can follow it. Let's see—what is the first thing to do?"

Tom considered a moment, going over the whole situation in his mind. He wished that he could have known the inside layout of the house. That might have aided him in maneuvering through it once inside. "Oh, well. Nothing to do about that," he mused.

He went on, talking to himself alone there in the woods, scratching the occasional doodle in the hard dirt. "It seems to me the first thing to do is to find out if the men are in the house, and if so, how many of them are there? To do that I've got to get closer and look in through a window. Now, how to get closer?"

He considered that problem from all sides. This involved moving back to his starting point from where he could see both house and lake.

"It will hardly do to approach from the lake shore," he reasoned. "If they have the motorboat and a dock, there must be a path from the house to the water. If there is a path people are likely to walk up or down it at any minute. Besides, the distance is too great and there is no shrubbery or anything to hide behind if necessary."

He looked back at the lake. "If man in the boat comes back unexpectedly, he would see me and alert the others. No, I can't risk approaching from the lake shore. I've got to work my way up to the house by going through the woods. That much is certain." To approach the house, and get close enough to see within, he needed to devise the next point in his plan. One thing at a time is a good rule, as his father used to say. "Poor dad! I do hope I can get his model and papers back for him."

Tom, who had been sitting on a log a few hundred feet from the lake, stood up. He was feeling rather weak and faint, and was at a loss to account for it, until he remembered that he had had no dinner the night before and only a meager meal for breakfast.

"And I'm not likely to get any," he remarked. "I'm not going to eat until I see who's in that house. Maybe I won't then, and where lunch will come from I don't know." He shook his head to clear it. This adventure was too important to be considered in the same breath with a meal.

Tom checked the contents of the small satchel he carried. Wishing that the had brought additional items, he close it and took a deep breath. It was time for action!

Cautiously Tom made his way forward, taking care not to make too much disturbance in the bushes. He had been on hunting trips and knew the value of silence in the woods.

There was no path to follow, but he had noted the position of the sun, and though it was now sinking lower and lower in the west, he could see the gleam of it through the trees, and knew in which direction from it lay the deserted mansion.

Tom moved slowly, and stopped every now and then to listen. The only sounds he heard were those made by the creatures of the woods—birds, squirrels and rabbits. In the distance he heard the call of a male elk. He crept forward for ten minutes, though only making slow progress, and he was just beginning to think that he might stand up to see how much farther it was to the house. He was just thinking that it must be near at hand when, through a fringe of bushes, he saw the old mansion. It stood in the midst of what had once been a fine park, but which was now overgrown with weeds and tangled briars. The paths that led to the house were almost out of sight, and would come in handy in disguising his final approach to the house.

"I guess I can sneak up there and take a look in one of the windows," thought the young inventor. He was about to advance, when he suddenly stopped. He heard someone or something coming around the corner of the mansion.

A moment later a man came into view, and Tom easily recognized him as another of those who had been in the automobile. The heart of the young inventor beat so hard that he was afraid the man would hear it. Tom crouched down in the bushes to keep out of sight.

The man evidently did not suspect the presence of a stranger. He cast sharp glances into the tangled undergrowth that fringed the house like a hedge, but saw nothing. He did not seek to investigate further and walked slowly on evidently circling the house but not straying more than a few feet from it.

Tom remained hidden for several minutes, and was about to proceed again, when the man reappeared. Then Tom saw the reason for it.

"He's on guard!" the lad said to himself. "He's doing sentry duty. I can't approach the house when he's there. I wonder why I didn't see him earlier?"

For an instant Tom felt a bitter disappointment. He had hoped to be able to carry out his plan. Now he would have to make a change.

"I'll wait until night," he thought. "Then I can sneak up and look in. The guard won't see me after dark. But it's going to be no fun to stay here, without anything to eat. Still, I've got to do it."

He remained where he was in the bushes. He noted that the man appeared on his rounds every eight to nine minutes, although Tom noted that occasionally he was gone for a longer period. He reasoned that the man would go into the mansion to confer with his confederates.

"If I only knew what was going on in there," thought Tom. "Maybe the men haven't got the model and papers here. But, if they haven't, why are they staying in the old house? I must get a look in and see what's going on. Lucky there are no shades to the windows. I wish I had some way of talking to dad right now."

While he sat and waited for night to fall, he considered what sort of portable two-way radio device he might built should he ever find himself in a similar situation. "Something using the new miniature vacuum tubes that were available along with one of the smaller batteries. Bet I could even make it small enough to carry in a backpack."

It seemed to Tom that the sun would never go down and bring on the dusk, but finally, crouching in his hiding place, Tom saw the shadows grow longer and longer, and finally the twilight of the woods gave way to darkness. Tom waited some time to see if the guard kept up the circuit, but with the approach of night the man seemed to have gone into the house. Tom saw a light gleam out from the lonely mansion. It came from a window on the ground floor.

"Now's my chance!" exclaimed the lad and, crawling from his hiding place, he advanced cautiously toward it.

Tom went forward only a few feet at a time, pausing almost every other step to listen. He heard no sounds, and was reassured. Nearer and nearer he came to the old house. The gleam of the light fell upon his face, and fearful that some one might be looking from the window, he shifted his course to come up from one side.

Slowly, very slowly he advanced, until he was right under the window. Then he found that it was too high up to let him in. He felt about for something to stand on. He located a large stone just feet away and quietly rolled it into position.

Softly he drew himself up inch by inch. He could hear the murmur of voices in the room. Now the top of his head was on a level with the sill. A few more inches and his eyes could take in the room and the occupants. He was scarcely breathing. Up, up he raised himself until he could look into the room, and the sight which met his eyes nearly caused him to lose his hold and topple backward.

Grouped around a table in a big room were the three men whom he had seen in the automobile. Thieves and attackers.

But what attracted his attention more than the sight of the men was an object on the table. It was the stolen model! The men were inspecting it, and operating it, as he could see. One of the trio had a bundle of papers in his hand, and Tom was sure they were the ones stolen from him. But there could be no doubt about the model of the turbine motor. There it was in plain sight. He had tracked the thieves to their hiding place.

Then, as he watched, Tom saw one of the men produce a

box from under the table, and the the model was placed inside. The papers were next put in and wadded papers added to prevent movement. A cover was nailed on. Then the men appeared to consult among themselves in low tones.

By their gestures Tom concluded that they were debating where to hide the box. One man pointed toward the lake, and another toward the forest. Tom was edging himself up a bit farther, in order to see better, and, if possible, catch their words. He overstretched and his foot slipped from the rock. Tom lost his grip on the sill and dangled from it, his feet a foot above the ground.

He dropped as silently as he could and believed he might have gone unnoticed.

A moment later, however, he heard someone approaching through the woods behind him, and a voice called out,

"You there! What are you doing? Get away from there!"

Rapid footsteps sounded, and Tom, in a panic, turned and fled.

An unknown pursuer was chasing after him.

TOM SWIFT and His Motorcycle

_____

CHAPTER XXIV

UNEXPECTED HELP

TOM RUSHED on through the woods. The lights in the room had temporarily blinded him. When it came to plunging into the darkness again, he could not see where he was going. He crashed full-tilt into a tree, and was thrown backward. Bruised and cut, he picked himself up and rushed off in another direction. Fortunately he stumbled onto some sort of a path, probably one made by cows. As his eyes recovered and adjusted to the darkness around him, he could dimly distinguish the trees on either side of him and was able to avoid them.

His heart, that was beating fiercely, calmed down after his first fright, and when he had run on for several minutes he stopped.

"That—that must—have been—the—the man—from the boat," panted our hero, whispering to himself. "He came back and saw me. I wonder if he's after me yet?"

Tom listened. He could hear his pursuer coming closer.

Tom reached into his bag and took out an object. He held it in his hand trying to decide if it would suit his needs.

He had almost no time to consider this as the man suddenly appeared before him.

"Got you, you little sneak!" the man growled and lunged clumsily forward, arms outstretched.

Tom held his device between them and flicked the switch with his thumb. As it came into contact with the man, the high voltage of his shocker coursed through the electrodes and into the man. He stiffened, making a gurgling noise and a short scream, then tumbled forward.

Tom could see in the twilight that the man lay twitching o n the ground, evidently unable to move. His eyes were wide as saucers and his jaw moved as if he was attempting to form words, words that he could not get out. He smelled alcohol on the man's breath.

Looking at his shock device, Tom remarked, "Wow. It really works great!" With that, he turned and fled into the undergrowth and was soon hundreds of yards away.

He stopped to listen again.

The only sound he could hear was the trill and chirp of the insects of the woods. The pursuit, which had lasted only a few minutes, was over. He wasn't certain how long the effects of his device might last, but it might quickly wear off and the pursuit be resumed at any moment. Tom was not safe yet, he thought, and he kept on.

"I wonder where I am? I need to find where my motorcycle is. I wonder what I had better do?" he asked himself.

Three big questions, and no way of settling them, Tom pulled himself up sharply. He had been carrying his shocker in his right hand in case it was required a second time. Now, he turned it off and replaced it into his bag.

"I've got to think this thing out," he resumed. "They can't find me in these woods tonight, that's sure, unless they get dogs. There was no sight or sound of those at the house. So I'm safe that far. But that's about all that is in my favor. I won't dare to go back to the house, even if I could find it in this blackness. They'll be on guard now. It looks as though I'm on my own. I'm afraid they may imagine the police are after them, and go away. If they do, and take the model and papers with them, I'll have an awful job to locate them again, and probably I won't be able to."

He suddenly wished that he had thought to involve the police in this matter. Now that he had seen the evidence, they would be able to make arrests and Barton Swift's property would be returned.

"That's the worst of it," he continued to himself. "Here I have everything right under my nose, and I can't do a thing. If I only had someone to help me, someone I could leave on guard while I went for the police. It's one against three—no, four. The man in the boat is back. Let's see what can I do?"

Then a sudden plan came to him.

"The lake shore!" he exclaimed, half aloud. "I'll go down there and keep watch. If they escape they'll probably go in the boat, for they wouldn't venture through the woods at night. That's it. I'll watch on shore, and if they do leave in the boat —" He paused again, undecided. "Why, if they do," he finished, "I'll sing out, and make such a row that they'll think the whole countryside is after them."

He reached into his bag and located the signal rocket. "I can send this up. Even before they get into their little boat. That may drive them back, or they may drop the box containing the papers and model, and run for it. If they do I'll be all right. I don't care about capturing them as long as I can get dad's model and papers back."

He felt more like himself, now that he had mapped out his

new plan.

"The first thing to do is to get back to the lake," reasoned Tom. "Let's see, if I assume that I ran in a straight line away from the house—that is, as nearly straight as I could—I should be able to turn around and go straight back. That should bring me back to the water. I'll do it."

But it was not so easy as Tom imagined. Several times he found himself in the midst of almost impenetrable bushes. He kept on, however, and soon had the satisfaction of emerging from the woods out on the shore of the lake. Getting his bearings as well as he could in the darkness, he moved down until he was near the deserted house. The light was still showing from the window, and Tom judged by this that the men had not taken fright and fled.

"I could sneak down and set their motorboat adrift," he thought. "That will prevent them leaving by way of the lake, anyhow. That's what I'll do!"

Very cautiously he advanced toward where he had seen the small craft put out. He took his shocker back out and switched it on. "I hope there is enough battery power remaining," he pondered. He was on his guard, for he feared the men would be on the watch. A moment later he reached the dock in safety, and was loosening the rope that tied the boat to the little dock when another thought came to him.

"Why set this boat adrift?" he reasoned. "It might make a good place for me to spend the rest of the night and could even be used to escape those men. I've got to stay around here until morning, and then I'll see if I can't get help. It is a fair trade. They have taken dad's model, and I'll take their boat."

Softly he got into the craft, and with an small oar which was kept in it to propel it in case the engine gave out, he poled it along the shore of the lake until he was some distance away from the dock.

That afternoon he had spotted a secluded place along the shore, a spot where overhanging bushes made a good hiding place. He rowed toward it in the small craft. A little later he had the boat completely out of sight, and Tom stretched out on the cushioned seats, pulling a tarpaulin over him. There he prepared to spend the rest of the night.

"They can't get away except through the woods now, which I don't believe they'll do," he thought, "and this is better for me than staying out under a tree. I'm glad I thought of it."

The youth, naturally, did not pass a very comfortable night, though his bed was not a half bad one. He fell into uneasy dozes, only to arouse, thinking the men in the old mansion were trying to escape. Then he would sit up and listen, but he could hear nothing save for his empty stomach and the occasional leaping fish. It seemed as if morning would never come, but at length the stars began to fade, and the sky seemed overcast with a filmy, white veil. Tom sat up, rubbed his smarting eyes, and stretched his cramped limbs.

"Oh, for a hot cup of coffee and a hot breakfast!" he exclaimed. "But not until I land these chaps where they belong. Now the question is, how can I get help to capture them?"

His hunger was forgotten as he considered his options. He stepped from the boat to a secluded spot on the shore. The craft, he noted, was well hidden. Even an approach from the water would require close proximity in order to see the hidden craft.

"I've got to go back to where I left my motorcycle, jump on that, and ride for aid," he reasoned. "Maybe I can get the charcoal-burner to go for me, while I come back and stand guard. I guess that would be the best plan. I certainly ought to be nearby. There is no telling when these fellows will skip out with the model, if they haven't gone already. I hate to leave, yet I've got to. It's the only way. I wish I'd done as dad suggested, and brought help. But it's too late for that."

Tom took a last look at the motorboat, which was a fine one. He wished it was his. Then he struck out through the woods. He had his bearings now, and soon found the place where he had left his machine. It had not been disturbed.

"I hope my birds haven't flown!" he exclaimed, and the thought gave him such uneasiness that he put it from him. Pushing his heavy machine ahead of him until he came to a good road, he mounted it, and was soon at the charcoal-burner's shack. There came no answer to his knock, and Tom pushed open the door. The old man was not in. Tom could not send him for help.

"Luck seems to be against me!" he murmured. "But I can get something to eat here, anyhow. I'm almost starved!"

He found the kitchen utensils, and made some coffee, and fried some bacon and eggs. Then, feeling much refreshed, he left enough money on the to pay for the food and started to go outside.

As Tom stepped to the door he was greeted by a savage growl that made him start in alarm. He froze in place.

"A dog!" he mused. "I didn't know there was one around."

He looked outside and there, to his dismay, saw a big, savage-appearing bulldog close to where he had left his motorcycle. The animal had been sniffing suspiciously at the machine.

"Good dog!" called Tom. "Come here!"

But the bulldog did not come. Instead the beast stood still, glowering at Tom. He showed his teeth to the youth and growled in a low tone.

"Wonder if the owner can be near?" mused the young inventor looking around. "That dog won't let me get my machine, I am afraid."

Tom spoke to the animal again and again the dog growled and showed his teeth. He next made a move as if to leap into the house, and Tom quickly stepped back inside and banged shut the door.

"Well, if this isn't the worst yet!" cried the youth to himself. "Here, just when I must be off, I am held up by that brute outside. Wonder how long he'll keep me a prisoner?"

Tom went to a window and peered out. No person had appeared and the lad rightly surmised that the bulldog had come to the cottage alone. The beast relieved itsself on the back tire of Tom's motorcycle. Then, looking around, it licked its chops. It appeared to be hungry, and this gave Tom a sudden idea.

"Maybe if I feed him, he'll forget that I am around and give me a chance to get away," he reasoned. "Guess I had better try that trick on him."

Tom looked around the cottage and found the remains of a steak dinner the owner had left behind. He picked up some of the bones and called the bulldog. The animal came up rather suspiciously. Tom threw him one bone, which he proceeded to crunch up vigorously.

"He's hungry right enough," mused Tom. "He'd probably like to sample my leg. But he's not going to do it—not if I can help it."

At the back of the cottage was a little shed, the door to which stood open. Tom threw a bone near to the door of this shed and then managed to throw another bone inside the place. The bulldog found the first bone and then disappeared after the second.

"Now's my chance," the young inventor told himself, and watching the door, he ran from the cottage toward his motorcycle. He made no noise and quickly shoved the machine into the roadway. Just as he turned on the power the bulldog came out of the shed, barking furiously.

"Too late! You've missed me!" said Tom grimly as the machine started, and quickly set the cycle speeding ahead, the cottage and the bulldog left behind.

The road was rough for a short distance and he had to pay strict attention to what he was doing.

"I've got to ride to the nearest village," he said. "It's a long distance. The men may escape before I can get help. But I can't do anything else. I can't tackle them alone, and there is no telling when the charcoal-burner may come back. I've got to make speed, that's all there is to it."

Out on the main road the lad sent his machine ahead at a fast pace. He was fairly humming along when, suddenly, from around a curve in the highway he heard the "honk-honk" of an automobile horn. For an instant his heart failed him.

"Please don't let that be the thieves! Maybe they have left the house, and are in their auto!" he whispered as he slowed down his machine, looking for an escape route.

The automobile appeared to have halted. As Tom came nearer the turn he heard voices. At the sound of one he started. The voice exclaimed, "Bless my spectacles! What's wrong now? I thought that when I got this automobile I would enjoy life, but it's as bad as that blessed and dratted motorcycle was for going wrong! Bless my very existence, but has anything happened?"

"Mr. Damon!" exclaimed Tom, for he recognized the eccentric individual of whom he had obtained the motorcycle.

The next moment Tom was in sight of a big touring car, containing, not only Mr. Damon, whom Tom recognized at once, but three other gentlemen.

"Oh, Mr. Damon," cried Tom, "will you help me capture a gang of thieves? They are in the deserted Harkness mansion in the woods, and they have one of my father's patent models! Will you help me, Mr. Damon?"

"Why, bless my top-knots," exclaimed the odd gentleman. "If it isn't Tom Swift, the young inventor! Bless my very happiness! There's my motorcycle, too! Help you? Why, of course we will. Bless my shoe-leather! Of course we'll help you!"

TOM SWIFT and His Motorcycle

―――

CHAPTER XXV

THE CAPTURE — GOODBYES

TOM'S STORY was soon told, and Mr. Damon quickly explained to his friends in the automobile how he had first made the acquaintance of the young inventor.

He made introductions of the gentlemen with him. "I have known Mr. Willoby for many a year and absolutely trust the man with my life. His two companions are new acquaintances, but are vouched for by Willoby.

"But how does it happen that you are trusting yourself to a car like this?" asked Tom. "I thought you were done with gasoline machines, Mr. Damon."

"I thought so, too, Tom, but, bless my batteries. My doctor insists that I must get out in the open air. I'm too old and stout to walk, and I can't run. The only solution was an automobile, for I never would dream of another motorcycle. It is a source of wonder that mine hasn't run away with you and killed you. But there! My automobile is nearly as bad. We went along very nicely yesterday, and now, just when I have a party of friends out, something goes wrong. Bless my liver! I do seem to have the worst luck!"

Tom lost no time in looking for the trouble. He found a simple loose wire in the ignition and soon had it fixed. Then, a sort of council of war was held.

"Do you think those scoundrels are still there?" asked Mr. Damon.

"I hope so," answered Tom.

"So do I," went on the odd character. "Bless my soul, but I want a chance to pummel them. Come, gentlemen, let's be moving. Will you ride with us, Tom, or on that dangerous motorcycle?"

"I think I'll stick to my machine, Mr. Damon. I can easily keep up with you. Besides. If you do not know where we are going it will be necessary for me to lead the way."

"Very well. Then we'll get along. We'll proceed until we get close to the old mansion, and then some of us will go down to the lake shore. The rest of us will surround the house. We'll catch those villains red-handed, and I hope we bag that tramp among them."

"I hardly think he is there," said Tom.

In a short time the auto and the motorcycle had carried the respective riders to the road through the woods. There the machines were left, and the party proceeded on foot. Tom had a revolver with him as did one member of Mr. Damon's party. The man explained he kept it more to scare dogs and animals that might block the road than for any other purpose. Tom gave his weapon to the other of Mr. Willoby's friends, and cut a stout stick for himself, an example followed by Mr. Damon and Mr. Willoby.

"A club for me!" exclaimed Mr. Damon hefting his rather short stick.

Cautiously they approached the house. Once they reached a point within seeing distance of it, they paused for a consultation. There seemed to be no one stirring about the old mansion, and Tom was fearful that the men had left. He knew they must have their auto secreted inside of the shed next to the house. Now, Tom considered that he should have attempted to disable that machine.

Mr. Willoby's two friends elected to go down to the shore of the lake on either side of the house to prevent any escape in that direction. The others, including Tom, were to approach from the wood side. When the two who were to form the water-side party were ready, one of them was to fire his revolver as a signal. Then Tom, Mr. Damon and the others would rush in.

The young inventor, Mr. Damon, and his friend Mr. Willoby went as close to the house as they considered prudent. Screening themselves in the bushes, they waited. They conversed in whispers, Tom giving more details of his experience with the patent thieves.

Suddenly, the silence of the woods was broken by someone advancing through the underbrush.

"Bless my gaiters, someone is coming!" exclaimed Mr. Damon in a hoarse whisper. "Can that be Munson or Dwight coming back?" He referred to the two men who had gone to the lake.

"Or perhaps the fellows are escaping," suggested Mr. Willoby. "Suppose we take a look."

At that moment the person approaching, whoever he was, began to sing. Tom started. He reached into his bag and withdrew his shocker.

"I'll wager that's Happy Harry, the tramp!" he exclaimed. "I know his voice."

Cautiously, Tom peered over the screen of bushes.

"Who is it?" asked Mr. Damon.

"It *is* Happy Harry! The tramp that caused me no little trouble," said Tom. "We'll get them all, now. He's going up to the house."

They watched the tramp. Apparently unaware of the eyes of the men and boy in the bushes, he kept on to a side door. He rapped out a sequence of knocks. Presently the door opened, and a man came out. Tom recognized him as Amberson Morse—the person who had dropped the telegram.

"About time you got here. Say, Burke," asked the man at the door, "have you taken the motorboat?"

"Motorboat? No," answered the tramp. "I just arrived here. I've had a hard time—nearly got caught in Swift's house the other night by that cub of a boy. Is the boat gone?"

"Yes. Anderson came back in it last night and saw some one looking in the window, but we thought it was only a farmer and chased after him. He hasn't come back and we were about to go searching for him. Probably got lost in the woods. Anyway, this morning the boat's gone. I thought maybe you had taken it for a joke."

"Not a bit of it! Something's wrong!" exclaimed Happy Harry looking around. "We'd better leave this place. I think the police are after us. That young Swift is too sharp for my liking. We'd better skip out while we can. I don't believe that was any farmer who looked in the window. Tell the others, get the stuff, and we'll leave."

From his place of concealment, Tom whispered, "They're here still. We're not too late!"

"I wonder if Munson and Dwight are at the lake yet?" asked Mr. Damon. "They ought to be—"

At that instant a pistol shot rang out. The tramp, after a startled glance around, started down the side porch steps.

The man in the doorway sprang out. Soon two others joined him. They ran to the front of the house.

"Who fired that shot?" cried Morse.

"Come on, Tom!" cried Mr. Damon, grabbing up his club and springing from the bushes. "Our friends have arrived!" The young inventor and Mr. Willoby followed him.

No sooner had they come into the open space in front of the house than they were seen. At the same instant, from the direction of the lake, came Mr. Munson and Mr. Dwight, guns drawn.

"We're caught!" cried Happy Harry.

He made a dash back to the house just as the third man, carrying a box, rushed out and collided with the tramp.

"There it is! The model and papers are in that box!" cried Tom. "Don't let them get away with it!"

The criminals were taken by surprise. With leveled weapons, the attacking party closed in on them. Mr. Damon raised his club threateningly.

"Surrender! Surrender!" he cried. "We have you! Bless my stars, but you're captured! Surrender!"

"It certainly looks so," admitted Amberson Morse. "I guess they have us, boys."

The man with the box made a sudden dash toward the woods, but Tom was watching him. In an instant he sprang at him, and landed on the fellow's back. The two went down in a heap, with the box tumbling from his grasp. Tom pressed his shocker against the man's side. As it went off, Tom could feel the tingle of the electrical shock making its way through both of their clothing. He shut it off before it might affect him.

When Tom arose he took possession of the precious box.

"I have it! I have it!" he cried. "I've got dad's model back!"

The man who had had possession of the box quickly arose, and before anyone could stop him, darted into the bushes. The shock had not incapacitated him.

"After him! Catch him! Bless my hat band, stop him!" shouted Mr. Damon.

Instinctively his friends turned to pursue the fugitive, forgetting, for the instant, the other criminals. The men were quick to take advantage of this, and had started for the dense woods when a shot rang out.

"Halt, in the name of the law!" Mr. Munson shouted and fired his gun into the air. The two main culprits halted and raised their hands in surrender.

"Pshaw! The man and the tramp got away from us!" cried Mr. Damon regretfully. "Let's see if we can't catch them. Come on, we'll organize a posse and run them down." He was eager for the chase, but his companions dissuaded him. Tom had what he wanted, and he knew that his father would be satisfied with the capture of the two men. The lad opened the box, and saw that the model and papers were safe.

"Let them go," advised the young inventor, and Mr. Damon reluctantly agreed to this, but insisted on seeing if the man Tom had knocked out was still there. Evidently, the combination of alcohol and Tom's electrical shock had incapacitated him for the entire evening. He was soon marched back to the shore and added to the group of thieves. There was no sign of Harry or his one accomplice.

"I guess we've seen the last of them," said the youth. "Now," said Mr. Damon, after it had been ascertained that no one was injured, and that the box contained all of value that had been stolen, "I suppose you are anxious to get back home, Tom, aren't you? Will you let me take you in my car? Bless my spark plug, but I'd like to have you along in case of another accident!"

The lad politely declined. With the valuable model and papers safely tied down on his motorcycle, he started for Shopton. Arriving at the first village after leaving the woods, Tom telephoned the good news to his father, and that afternoon was heading safely for home.

Tom stopped by the Shopton police station where he received a great surprise.

Standing in front of the desk was Happy Harry. Anger flared in Tom's mind and, before he knew it, a fist had lashed out and caught Harry directly on the chin.

It had two immediate effects. One was that the beard Tom had once believed to be fake proved to be just that. It practically flew from the man's face and landed more than five feet away.

The second effect was that it knocked the man clean off of his feet and onto his back.

Tom felt the anger leaving his body, but went back on guard when the third, totally unexpected reaction happened.

Happy Harry began to laugh.

He raised himself up to his knees and, holding up a hand to stop Tom from hitting him again, stood up to face the youth.

He rubbed his jaw, thoughtfully and moved it back and forth as if trying to find if it still worked. Satisfied, he held out his right had to Tom.

"Inspector Harry Greene, Mister Swift. At your service." With his tramp speech gone, Tom realized that he had a slight British accent. "I must rather apologize for all of the brouhaha that has occurred. You see," he said reaching into his jacket pocket and drawing out his wallet, "I am an inspector with Scotland Yard but attached to your own War Department." He showed Tom his identification.

"I have been working as a sort of double agent. My real

duties and loyalties lie, of course, with Britain and the United States, but I have been a part of the gang who have been trying to steal your father's invention. His—" he lowered his voice and nodded to Tom, "—new engine?"

Astonished, Tom simply stood there, mouth agape.

"But, you're the one who broke my motorcycle!"

Smiling, Greene admitted it was he who had done just that. "But, wouldn't it have been far worse if one of the other members of our little team did it? They might not have grabbed some piece so obviously replaceable. They might have even caused you great harm and then taken the model of the engine. Hmm?"

Tom had to admit to himself that it did make sense.

Greene explained how his actions were meant to make it difficult for the thieves to locate Tom. "I'm sorry to say that I failed in that and that you were put through quite an experience." He had also allowed the third man to escape from the Harkness house. "I may be required to continue my ruse, so I needed to let at least one of them escape. Hopefully they will not tumble to my plans."

He explained that he was working on behalf of the U.S. government. "We are involved in defeating a ring of industrial spies operating to provide an unfriendly nation with American and British technological instruments. This was an excellent opportunity to insinuate one of our own into the gang."

"Did dad know—" he began asking.

"He never knew a thing about our actions," the agent told Tom. "His invention was used to flush out our trio of villains. We couldn't have your father knowing what was happening. He is a great inventor, but your father is not a good actor. We knew that and acted accordingly."

"Must you tell him? He will feel that he has been made a fool of, you realize," Tom asked the man.

"Would you?" The agent looked quizzically at Tom.

Finally, Tom shook his head. "Dad is a wonderful man. He already believes that he placed my life in jeopardy. I don't think knowing all this would have any positive result. Just so that I know, what about the others?"

"Others? Oh, you mean others you encountered along the way?" he asked the youth.

"Yes. That others."

"Well, there was only one other agent in the field of which I am aware. That hunter you encountered after our first meeting. A G-man. I was curious to see that you did not recognize him as being Mr. Munson as well. Between myself and him we needed to stall your initial journey for long enough so that I could get back to join the others in their touring automobile. I am sorry if I did any permanent damage to your cycle."

Tom left the police station wondering just how far the entire affair had really stretched. Little did he realize that it would all come back to affect him in his next adventure.

He returned to the Swift home to a celebration and great meal.

Barton Swift lost no time in fully protecting his invention by patents. As for the unprincipled men who made an effort to secure it, they had so covered up their misdeeds that there was no way of prosecuting them, nor could any action be held against Elrod & Drimble, the unscrupulous lawyers.

In the end, the men had been released from jail and disappeared.

"Well," remarked Mr. Swift to Tom, a few nights after the recovery of the model, "your motorcycle certainly did us good service. Had it not been for it I might never have gotten back my invention."

"It did come in handy," agreed the young inventor. "There's that motorboat, too. I wish I had it. I doubt that those fellows will ever come back for it. It was turned it over to the county authorities, and they have charge of it now." He wondered what he might do if he could convince them to sell him that boat. Time would tell.

"I certainly had some odd adventures since I got this machine from Mr. Damon," concluded Tom.

THE END

Tom Swift will next be seen in his forthcoming story
TOM SWIFT and HIS MOTORBOAT
A new adventure for today's science minded boys.

This story will be available from all reputable booksellers and may be borrowed from most public libraries.

CPSIA information can be obtained
at www.ICGtesting.com
Printed in the USA
FSOW04n2335211216
28754FS